The Gum Chews

A REASONABLE AMOUNT OF TROUBLE

JoAnna Rowe

THE GUM CHEWS
A Reasonable Amount of Trouble

© 2024, JoAnna Rowe

Print ISBN: 979-8-35095-611-5
eBook ISBN: 979-8-35095-612-2

For Jack.

CHAPTER 1

PICKLES

Today feels like every day—only worse. I woke up the same bitter pickle, sloshing around in my salty brine, when my dad came out of nowhere and shook the jar. My world is spinning, and now I race against time to deliver the worst news ever.

My Oxford shoes click along the hallway tile. They slide and squeak around corners. I steer my way to the school's cafeteria and shift my eyes toward students laughing at me.

When I punch the cafeteria doors, an old memory punches back. A garbage disposal full of feelings churns behind my scowl. I wasn't always this kid. Everything changed when I met a man named Sam Spade on the day my dad disappeared.

CHAPTER 2

FRANK JR.

I learned my dad disappeared five years ago on my sixth birthday. But before that, the simple birthday celebration made for a nice memory. Half-inflated balloons dangled with mild intentions from the mismatched chairs surrounding our small dining table. The splattered remains of my cake lay in ruins across a plastic birthday tablecloth. Six burnt candles resembled buried toy soldiers within crumbled chocolate.

I was another kid named Frank Jr. then. Little "Frank the Innocent" sitting at his dwindling birthday party soon to become "Frank the Forgotten." I can't believe I waited so long to choose a better name.

Grandpa Gilbert entered the living room where I sat like a chocolate-stuffed zombie letting my mom clean my face. She liked to fuss with my cheeks when she was nervous. I watched her closely, wondering why she was worried on my birthday.

Grandpa told her to stop and flashed me the playful grin he saved for mischief. He held up a gift the size of a video game. It was tightly wrapped in his finished crossword puzzle page from the newspaper. A small green bow was smashed in the corner.

"Happy birthday, kiddo," he said and handed it to me.

I ripped open the paper. A tight smile spread across my face, pinching my cheeks to my ears.

"A movie with no color," I said, holding my fake smile.

My mom and grandma started grumbling. The old man's face was bright with laughter.

Grandpa gave me something that got him into trouble, and he was loving it. I knew that meant I would love it too. I gave a real smile with what teeth I had.

I couldn't read well enough yet, so I picked out letters for the words everyone was repeating. I whispered the strange names that would soon change my life. "Humphrey Bogart. The Maltese Falcon."

Grandpa Gilbert kneeled to my level with a slight grunt. "Quiet down, ladies," he said. "Don't be silly. This movie is not inappropriate. It's just what he needs." Grandpa grew serious and looked me in the eyes. "I see you, kiddo. You notice things others don't. You remember things most forget. You observe the world deeper than children do."

"Is something wrong with me?" I asked.

"No," Grandpa said in a way that sounded like he was crying and chuckling at the same time. "You are like I was as a kid. You get an itch right behind your nose when you can't solve something, and it won't stop until you figure it out. Am I right?"

My eyes grew wide. "You get an itchy nose too?"

He frowned. "I used to. I wasn't the same after the war—"

"After your warhorse, Icabum, died?" I interrupted.

"I wasn't the same after many friends I loved died." He coughed away his frown. "But I know the skill when I see it."

"Skill for what?"

Grandpa grabbed my shoulder. "To be a detective," he said and smiled. "Maybe the world's greatest detective."

"Really?" I'd heard the word before, but I didn't know what it meant. "But what's a detective?" I asked.

"It's someone who puts the pieces together to solve a problem." His smile grew. He tapped the DVD in my hands. "Let me introduce you to Sam Spade."

CHAPTER 3

BUTTERBEAN

A high voice hollers my name. The cafeteria door swings closed and smacks my face before I can enter the hall. I rub my cheek and look toward the voice. My English teacher runs at me, waving a paper. Ms. Butterbean calls my name again as I hurry to make my escape. I don't have time for her. I need to find my friends.

"Icabum Plum!" Ms. Butterbean says my new name in a song. She holds the door. Her lipstick has smeared onto her teeth, and there is a coffee stain on her collar.

"Oh, hello, Ms. Butterbean," I say dryly. "Did you need something?"

"Yes!" she replies, her eyes bright. "I entered your last creative essay on how holistic medicine could have benefited Dr. Doolittle's animals into a national writing contest, and you made it into the finals!"

I scrunch my face. "You did what?"

"I know, I know. I should have asked, but it was the last day to enter, so I went for it. And look at it! You're in the finals. Icabum, you deserve this. You are a very special writer. You see things so differently."

"Well, hooray," I say while pushing on the cafeteria door. I only have thirty minutes during lunch to discuss with my friends how to get out of the worst thing to ever happen.

"Wait, wait, hold on. It's the last day before spring break, and I won't see you. I need to explain the rules. You don't have a lot of time."

She's right. I don't. I let out a breath. "What is it I need to do?"

"You need to write under two thousand words about what skills you think children should learn."

I scoff. "What? I have to write another essay?"

"If you do this, I will give you extra credit for any class papers you write for the rest of the year."

"I don't need extra credit. I always get an A."

"Well then, do it for the $200."

I wince and look up. $200. The thought of money stirs a fresh emotion I tuck behind my stern look. Money could help my problem. I clear my throat. "When would I get paid?"

Ms. Butterbean chuckles. "I love your confidence. The essay is due the day you return from spring break. The winner will be announced a few days later."

I sag like a day-old party. I'd get the money too late. This doesn't help me right now. "Sorry, Ms. Butterbean. I have a busy week. I can't."

"Well, I'll give your mom a call—"

"No! Wait." I grip my forehead. I can't let my mom know about a project like this before spring break. I already have enough going on to have her pestering me about it. "Fine. I'll figure it out. Just . . . don't tell my mom."

"Excellent and good luck!" Ms. Butterbean says. "Oh, and you better take off that fedora before Principal Curd sees. He's warned you a few times about wearing hats at school."

I reach up and pull my favorite hat from my head. It's the same fedora Sam Spade wore. I always wear this one when there is a problem to solve.

CHAPTER 4

SPADE

Sam Spade. Humphrey Bogart. The Maltese Falcon. Detective. These were only words until Grandpa Gilbert put the DVD in that day and pressed play. The words then became my reality. I didn't blink. I didn't speak. I no longer noticed the lack of color. It was a pencil sketch that came to life. I focused on what the people were doing instead. How they spoke, how they moved.

Humphrey Bogart was the actor who played Sam Spade, but I couldn't tell where the man ended and the character began. He spoke in a way that made me listen. He moved with thoughtful steps.

And his clothes . . . his clothes! Sam Spade wouldn't be the same in the cartoon tee and sweats Frank Jr. had on that day. He dressed for the business of being a detective—a perfect suit and tie, topped with a brimmed hat called a fedora purposefully placed at a tilt on his head. In the end, Sam Spade solved the great mystery of the missing Maltese Falcon statue.

The definition of a detective was clear. It was the itch I got. Sam Spade felt the same need to find the answer to a mystery. Being a detective was the stuff that dreams were made of, and I dreamed of being like Sam Spade: the greatest detective in the world. All I had to do was find a great mystery to solve. That would be hard. Nothing more exciting than a lost turtle happened in my boring, little town of Circle's End.

My favorite memory ended with me clapping. I return to that moment often, savor it, feel the ache of that old wide smile, and let the clap of my hands slow in beat, delaying the terrible memory that followed right after.

"I can't wait to show this to Dad," I said when the movie ended. My brows pinched together. "Wait, wasn't Dad supposed to be home from his trip already?"

Grandpa Gilbert frowned at his hands. He looked across the room to the kitchen, where Grandma Ginger hugged my mom. He took a deep breath. "Come sit next to me, kiddo." When I followed, he continued, "I don't know how to say this, so I'll just say it. Your parents are getting a divorce."

I didn't understand the word, so I stared.

He scratched his gray facial hair. "It means your pa's not going to be living here."

"But he told me he'd be here for my birthday," I said, scrunching my face. "Where is he now?"

My dad said selling insurance involved a lot of traveling. I was used to him missing special days, but I wondered what was different about this divorce thing that kept him away.

"We're not sure, to be honest," Grandpa replied.

"Can I call him?" I asked.

Grandpa held his frown. "I don't want to speak ill of your pa, and I hold myself to not saying anything at all if I don't have something nice to say, but he . . . he has a way of only thinking of himself, and when he does, he can be hard to find."

"Hard to find?" I repeated to myself.

"But, hey, do you know who you can call anytime?" Grandpa didn't wait for my answer. "Me, kiddo. I'm here for you anytime you need me. Okay?"

I didn't reply then and not again when Grandpa asked me how I was feeling. He patted me on the back and headed to the kitchen to get my mom. Her wide eyes were on me with a classic mama-bear stare.

I scratched my nose. The itch was there. I jolted from the couch and charged to my room. My family called after me, but I ignored them to let thoughts play in my mind. Grandpa said my dad was hard to find. I locked my bedroom door and pressed my back against it. I had my great case.

"I'm going to find Dad," I said.

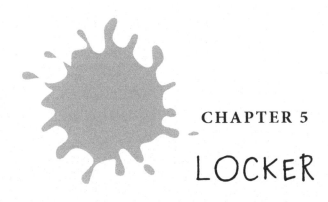

CHAPTER 5

LOCKER

I placed my fedora hat back on my head when Ms. Butterbean was out of sight and pushed through the cafeteria doors into the jungle of shameless, reckless youth. Survival of the fittest at its finest. Hundreds of kids perform to be the best at being cool. Some cheat with money. Some lose with a few unsavory whispers. I'd rather be a director than an actor.

In the corner, my best friend lifts a finger to get my attention, like I can't see his tall body towering over the others. He frowns. I haven't seen him since this morning when he found me hiding inside my locker. I pinch my eyes closed when the feelings from that time seep through my hard shell.

My forehead was rested against the inside of my school locker. My groan echoed around me. "I'm not going. Nope. No way," I had said, thinking about the horrible news my mother told me the night before. My dad is back, and I'm being sent to his house for spring break.

Sometimes emotions hit me with the feeling of eating too many cocktail weenies at a baby shower. I will crouch inside my locker to unzip that hard-boiled side of myself everyone sees and try to breathe.

In front of people, I can't be a flopping fish out of water, a tumbling rock down a hill, or a twirling kite without a string. I keep sharp. A good detective is tightly tailored.

Before I exited my locker this morning, I reminded myself that I was Icabum Plum, the greatest detective Circle's End has ever known. Seeker of truth and justice 24/7. The toothpick carving plaque from the crevices of society.

"Be the bitter coffee without the cream," I repeated one of my grandpa's tips.

The locker door rattled with a knock. "Who did it this time?" asked my best friend, Enzo Lemon, in his signature low mumble.

Enzo is the tallest eleven-year-old I've ever seen. He stands out, and he hates it. Middle school is a puberty lottery. Each month, you hope your number is called. Meanwhile, big, hairy Vikings and half-evolved amphibians walk over shapeless amoebas waiting to grow. Enzo and I are on opposite sides in many ways. We fill in for what the other is missing, and that's what makes us great together. There's no other partner I'd rather have.

I slapped my cheek and cleared my throat, readying myself to make my exit. "The usual ignoramus," I replied. The lie wasn't easy.

A *rattle*, a *thunk*, and the locker door swung open. I squinted into the invading light and nodded my thanks. My best friend frowned, reading something I'd left lingering on my face. The tracksuit his parents paid a fortune for crunched as he crossed his arms. Thick, shiny hair covered his green eyes like someone sat a black bowl upside down on top of his head.

"Your house phone is broken," he mumbled. "All okay?"

I brushed off my favorite gray three-piece suit, adjusted my bowtie, and squeezed out of the locker with my chin angled. My classic black fedora hat was tilted over one eye.

"No. Not okay," I told Enzo. "We need to call an emergency Gum Chew meeting." I found my confident tone without all the squeaks. Detective talk requires a tight jaw, a gravel tone, and little movement of the lips. It's harder than it seems with the kazoo recently growing in my throat. Kids shoved past me on the way to class. I caught my stumble.

"Meeting? Bad news?" Enzo said, lifting a big, steadying hand to my shoulder.

I straightened my waistcoat. "Remember when Martha Sesame spent the whole day walking around with a cheese slice stuck to her shoe, and then she kicked it off onto Pepe Bucatini's sandwich, which he ate and threw up all over our front row on picture day?"

Enzo nodded.

"Worse than that."

CHAPTER 6

EMERGENCY

My other friends surround Enzo at the table where he sits in the cafeteria. "Good. They're all here," I say to myself.

The Gum Chews are a band of Don Kiwi Middle School's sharpest minds, a coalition of servants to this town's safety, each trained by me in the art of investigation. The dictionary calls us names like sleuthhounds, gumshoes, and shamuses, but townspeople murmur that we're irritants and pains. That's good. Because when it comes to truth and justice, the Gum Chews are no one's friend.

"We don't have a lot of time," I say by way of greeting them. "Roll call, Gum Chews, and let's get right to it."

"Same three people every time, Ick," Tyrone Chokeberry says with a flat tone. He gnaws on the required gum at all Gum Chew meetings. It helps us think.

"You won't allow anybody else in," adds his brother, Tyler, another gum-chewing gumshoe.

I roll my eyes. "Quality, not quantity."

Candidates lately have been incompetent. One kid wouldn't take my entry essay, another refused to search a trash can for the evidence test, and the most recent applicant got lost in the bathroom.

The Chokeberrys, however, are the two best associates any detective could have. The brothers are only nine months apart in age, so both are in sixth grade with me.

Tyrone sits beside Enzo on the bench, grinning at a group of kids passing by. He has the charisma of those YouTubers who make millions of dollars for doing nothing substantial. People love him, which makes Tyrone my top spy.

Tyler, the younger of the two, sits on the floor against the wall with a laptop on his legs. He's my shadow, always dressed in tight black clothes. The boy can weave in and out of any room without being seen. Plus, Tyler's the greatest engineer I know, maybe even better than his father.

"All meetings need structure," I say, crossing my arms over my chest. "And I won't ignore the fact that you still haven't watched the movies I suggested. Did you at least read the Cliff Notes I wrote?" I wave a hand when they scrunch their faces in rightful shame. "For another time," I add. "We have more pressing matters. You've all read the missive Enzo passed out."

Enzo stares.

I point at the three pages of photocopies in his hand. "The *report* I wrote detailing the current crisis. Thoughts? Ideas? Philosophies? Prophecies? I'll take anything at this point."

Tyrone frowns. "Is it really that bad to go to your dad's house for a week?"

I stare blankly at the dirty cafeteria tiles. "Yes," is all I can say.

CHAPTER 7

DAD

For a year after he left, Dad sent me eight postcards from eight countries. Each said the same thing. How was I? Was I being good? He didn't know when he'd see me, but he would try to visit as soon as he could. Work kept him busy. He'd write at his next stop.

After Mom sat me down to talk about the divorce, I understood what it meant. My dad didn't want to be married to my mom. When I asked why Dad was traveling to other countries when he never did before, my mom said it must have been for work. My detective itch grew stronger.

I made my first case file using a large sheet of green construction paper folded in half. The case name labeled on the front said *Dad*. Inside, I stored the postcards and a map where I logged all the locations.

I worked my first big case the best a seven-year-old could. I rode my bike to the sheriff's station to listen to Sheriff Bass's radio at the front desk for clues. They didn't mind since I offered to sweep the floor while I hung out. When I got bored, I visited the post office next door to help my mom's friend, Judy, stamp envelopes while I waited for incoming mail.

I watched dozens of old black-and-white detective movies that Grandpa sent me. I memorized every word as I crafted my skills.

In a notebook I labeled *Tips*, I collected my favorite Sam Spade lessons I learned:

- Enter through back doors instead of front doors to study people's surprise reactions.

- Use the tip of your shoe instead of your hands to check evidence on the ground because it is hard to squat in tight pants.

- Squint like the light's too bright. It looks cool.

Grandpa gave me movies about other private investigators too. I watched *Kiss Me Deadly* at least ten times. It was about an investigator in 1955 hunting for a mysterious box called The Great Whatsit. No matter how many times I watched it, I couldn't figure out what was inside the box. It drove me crazy! But there was a more pressing mystery to solve.

My case file was tattered from nights of review. I sat at my desk in the ill-fitting Sunday-best suit I'd worn every day that year and grown too tall for. I looked at the front of my dad's postcards and flipped them over with a sigh.

"Every detail is a story," I whispered. It was one of the tips I learned.

I studied the American flag stamps on each postcard. I thought Dad must have traveled with a pack of them from home. The post office sold the same ones. My eyes snagged on the postmark stamp. I blinked. Judy at the post office said the postmark stamp was put on outgoing mail. All my dad's postcards were postmarked in Savannah, Georgia.

I looked up. "Dad didn't send these from different countries. He's . . . here."

A soft knock on my door slapped me out of thought. My mom stood in the doorway of my room. Her body was a shadow silhouette, but a faint early morning light crossed her face. From my detective studies, I learned that I needed to pay attention to people, especially their body language and how they shift their eyes. My mom's eyes were puffy, but she smiled. A smile like she smashed her finger and was trying not to scream.

"Sweetheart," she said. The word was weighted with the mountain of love she always fills it with. "There is someone here to see you."

Before I could reply, a broader figure as tall as my mom entered the room.

"Hey, Junior," said a deep voice. That name and that voice introduced my worst memory.

I squinted. "Dad?" I jumped to my feet and sprinted to him. I remembered my notes and stopped before I hugged him. My detective itch pushed me to solve the mystery. My bubbly gut told me I'd done it, but I hoped I was wrong. *Please be wrong,* I said to myself before I asked, "How was France?" I looked past him. My mom was gone.

Dad cleared his throat. "Nice," he replied, "but I'm happy to be back in the States."

I'd trained for hours in front of a mirror to be like Sam Spade and not blink. Liars can't beat a hard stare. Dad wouldn't meet my eyes.

"I asked your mom if you can stay with me for the weekend," he said. "Go pack a bag."

I finally blinked. "Stay with you?"

"Yeah, we can hang out and get caught up."

The questions hardening my judgment whooshed away as I rushed to pack a bag. Did I really care where he had been? I had set out to find my dad. Case closed.

"Change your clothes," Dad added as he left my room.

I paused at my closet. "But I always wear these clothes."

"You look silly. Throw on some sweats and a shirt so we can play ball later."

My hustle slowed. This suit was who I wanted to be, and I hated sports. I shook off the sludge slowing me down and undressed. He didn't know that. Then again, he didn't know much about me.

Once ready, I scampered out of our little apartment and jumped in my dad's truck. We drove for hours. My dad mostly nodded to my yapping, but he never talked much before.

Three hours later, we crossed into Savannah, Georgia. I grew quiet, remembering my dad's postcards. "You live in Savannah," I said.

His brows pulsed. "How do you know that?"

It wasn't the itch that returned but a churning in my stomach. My lips dipped to one side. "A guess."

Lush green trees framed cookie-cut houses. Wide-open streets hugged yards filled with children playing. Curiosity pressed me against the window as my dad pulled into a driveway at the end of a cul-de-sac. A home resembling a blue gingerbread house peaked over a garden of bright yellow flowers.

"Is this your house?" I asked.

He nodded without looking my way. "It belongs to Betty and me."

Before I could ask who Betty was, the front door swung open. A young woman with a baby wrapped in her arms walked out onto the front porch. The woman's lips parted in a nice smile when she saw me.

"Junior, that is Betty and your brother," my dad said. "His name is also Frank." Dad's words drifted away, and their meaning settled over me.

My face slacked like it was made of slime. "*Whose* baby is that?"

"He's mine and Betty's son."

"And his name is . . ."

"Frank, since you just go by Junior."

I flashed my teeth. I have a brother with *my* name.

"Is this why you lied to everyone?" *To me*, I added silently. My neck flushed with fire.

Dad winced. "Your mom knows about the baby."

The sting of my mom knowing caught my words, but I pushed through. "No, that you've been here all year. You were never in other countries. I noticed your postcards were postmarked in Savannah."

I watched Dad's cheeks paint red. He sighed. "Does your mom know?"

"I don't think so."

"Good," he said.

My detective training marked his shifting eyes as textbook lying.

"I was sent to the mountains," he continued. "The reception was bad, so I thought it would be exciting for you to get postcards from different countries. It was to distract you from the divorce. Betty sent them for me. She is very excited to meet you—"

I stopped listening to his lies. At some point, Dad left the car, abandoning me again. I solved my great case, and my reward was learning my dad wasn't hard to find. He only found a new family and replaced me with another Frank.

A case that cut this deep would have made any half-rate Scooby-Doo detective quit, but I took that day as another chapter in the Sam Spade training guide. A lesson titled *How to put the hard-boiled in hard-boiled detective.*

I wrote in my pocket notebook and sniffed back a different type of itch, one behind my eyes that stirred a tear loose.

Hard-boiled is knowing no one will give you the truth. Hard-boiled is punching through the lies. Hard-boiled is sealing up your heart to keep it from getting crushed.

I didn't want to admit my heart was already broken, but I sealed it up anyway. That's what greatness is: puttying your cracks to keep yourself together.

I stared out the car window at my dad's new life. The next great case was somewhere waiting to be solved, my own Maltese Falcon that would help me forget the *Dad* case.

CHAPTER 8

FILM FESTIVAL

Tyrone leans forward and pats my shoulder to get my attention. "Don't go to your dad's house and stay with Enzo."

Enzo frowns beside him on the bench. He bounces a ball. His face grows blotchy red like it did earlier when I told him the news that I was being forced to leave.

"His parents are gone," I grumble and pat a wrinkle on my suit like I can rub away the fire burning under my skin. "My dad already bought the bus ticket. But this is bigger than that. Did you read my notes?" I point at the report. "I can't go. I found my great case."

A brief smirk flashes on my face. To teach me responsibility, Mom signed an agreement with Grandpa's old war buddy, Farney Fig, to have me be his stock boy on the weekends at the Fit and Flare Tailor Shop. In payment, I get credit to buy suits. Best job ever!

Last Sunday, I cruised down the backroad of my little town on my bike and skidded to a stop in front of the small brick tailor shop. In the front window, there were two mannequins I dressed. I parked my bike, dusted off my slim navy suit jacket, and then froze at a note on the door.

Icabum,

I have a doctor's appointment.

Take the day off. Don't worry. You'll still get credit.

See you next Saturday. –F. Figs

P.S. Those magazines you like are in the recycle bin.

I grinned and popped a fresh ball of Bubble-Yo gum in my mouth. "Paid for not working," I said. "Ain't that the dream." I went around the building to the recycling bin in the alley. A stack of *Tailor Made* magazines was piled inside. I eagerly yanked them out and riffled through them as I walked back to my bike.

"Holiday Style" and "Winter Wear" were the headlines for the first two magazines. "Ugh, they're old," I grumbled. As I crossed onto the sidewalk, someone collided with me, and my magazines flew out of my hands.

I cleared my throat. "Oh, hi, Sheriff."

Sheriff Bass's thick, brown mustache ruffled when he said, "Sorry there, Fra—Icabum. I didn't see you." The formidable man's body towered over me as he tilted his hat in greeting.

"The curse of being short," I said with a shrug.

Sheriff rumbled a deep laugh. "Let me help you with those." He picked up a few magazines and handed them to me. "Keeping out of trouble?" His baritone voice sounded like when I talked into my desk fan.

"Yes, sir."

He grunted a little as he lifted from a squat. "Do you have plans for spring break? Any lost things still need finding?"

"No, sir." I sulked. "Nothing illegal ever happens in this sleepy town."

Sheriff Bass leaned down to my level. "Then we're doing our job." He winked and sauntered off.

I scratched my frown. "Sir!" I called out. "Did you get my note?"

Sheriff turned back. "I did." A smile inched up his cheek. "It's not in my jurisdiction to force Greta to change the sign outside her house."

I looked down at my feet with a snarl, squeezed the magazines tight in my hands, and then lifted my eyes back to him. "It's criminal, sir."

His mustache shifted. "She's only offering neighbors the items listed on the sign for free. Greta's cat had kittens, and she wants to get rid of some supplies." He knew I was right. That was why he hesitated with his next words. "Tools and two squash and kittens."

"But the sign doesn't say that! She wrote *Tools 2 Squash Kittens*. Sir, I'm having trouble believing it's a grammatical error. She's a teacher! Did you get a warrant?"

Sheriff chuckled. I didn't see what was so funny. "I have an idea, Icabum," he said. "Why don't you go pick up her squash and then see if she scratches out those words on the sign?"

I chewed on it for a moment. As I did, Sheriff patted me on the shoulder and walked away.

"Okay," I called after him. "But if you don't see me around town, you know where to check first."

Sheriff looked over his shoulder and winked.

I groaned and reached down for the last magazine on the ground. The others in my hand spilled again. I pinched my eyes shut for a breath and returned to picking up the magazines. One was flipped open to a man wearing a gray suit and a herringbone-pattern sweater vest. I dog-eared the corner and followed the *Trend Alert* article titled "Not Your Grandfather's Herringbone." The article was so good that I sat down on the sidewalk. My dress pants were too tight to sit crisscross applesauce, so I crossed my shiny black Oxford loafers in front of me.

Two pages later, I got up, satisfied and yearning for a herringbone sweater vest. I tossed the magazines in my bike basket. The back of one magazine faced me upside down. I blinked and raced to pick it back up. A Maltese Falcon statue glistened beneath bold print on the glossy back cover.

10th Annual Classic Film Festival at Old Town's Galagala Convention Center. Saturday, April 13th. Doors open at 1:00 p.m. For all you detectives out there, solve the featured case to win $1,000 plus this trophy. Don't forget to dress the part!

"Next weekend!" I croaked.

My heart thundered as I flipped over the magazine to make sure it wasn't an old issue. I gasped. It wasn't! I looked around like someone might be punking me. My mouth dried up. I could win a Maltese Falcon statue just like in the movie. I raced home as fast as I could to call my grandpa and ask him to take me. This was it. My great case.

"We have to go to the film festival," I say to my friends, meeting each of their stares. "We could win an actual Maltese Falcon! I want it. I need it." The last three words fall to a whisper.

"But what about your mom?" Tyrone says.

I wince and shake my head. The words won't come out.

CHAPTER 9

LIGHTS OUT

When I arrived home yesterday evening after hanging out at Enzo's house, I found my mom sitting at our kitchen table. She moved her hands away from her face when she heard me.

I squinted to adjust to the dim lighting. "Mom, why's it so dark—?" The light didn't turn on when I flicked the switch. I tried it again.

"Hey, sweetheart," Mom said. I felt an icy chill creep up my spine at the tone. It left a taste like coffee sweetened with too much sugar. "Come sit with me."

I didn't sit. "What's wrong?" I said instead. "Why doesn't the light work?"

"That's not important. Sit, please."

I obeyed slowly. She rubbed something away from my cheek. I held her hand with a stern stare. "What is it, Mom?"

She pulled her hand away. "One more day until spring break . . ."

I sat taller. "I can't wait for Grandpa to get here." A rare grin washed over my face at the thought of the film festival. We agreed not to tell Mom where we were going. She thinks the old movies we watch are a bad influence on me.

A little hiccup got trapped in Mom's throat. "Grandpa can't come anymore," she said softly.

"What? Why?" My grandparents regularly make the four-hour drive from Florida since they moved out of this town last year. They're retired now. They have nothing else to do.

Her face slacked. "He has . . . appointments."

I snarled at the table. That wasn't like my grandpa. He never let me down. He knew how much the film festival meant to me. How was I going to get there now?

Mom pulled out a slip of paper from her purse. "The diner is always super busy during spring break, so I'm needed for extra shifts. I was going to get Grandma's friend from bingo to watch you at night—"

"Mrs. Tarp! I can't get her perfume smell off the couch from the last time she visited." I slumped in the chair with a groan.

"Calm down," she said. "I don't need to ask Mrs. Tarp because . . . your dad's back at home and offered to help."

I flinched away like I'd been slapped. "Offered to *help*?" I sank so far in my seat that I was nearly a puddle. "Another overnight? When is he picking me up?" My stays in Savannah had grown short and far between over the years.

"It's not an overnight trip this time. You will be there the 13th through the 17th—"

"13th!" The film festival date. My sight spun. I had to spend all week with my dad, miss the film festival, miss my friends. "Tell him to stay home. I'll sleep at Enzo's—" I frowned.

Enzo's parents were super rich and traveled a lot. They were already gone for the month. Enzo was alone with his nanny, Paoula. He was going to the festival with my grandpa and me. This was a blow to both of us. I needed to know what was going on with Grandpa Gilbert. What was so important that he couldn't come? He would never abandon me. He promised.

"No, you can't stay at Enzo's without his parents there." Mom lifted the paper she was holding. "And your dad's not picking you up this time. He bought you a bus ticket."

I looked between her and the ticket. "I have to go to him?"

"It took some considering, but your dad said he used to take the bus alone all the time at your age."

I smashed my face against the table. He'd likely send Betty and the kid to pick me up from the bus station.

Mom leaned forward and rubbed my hand. "Your dad's making an effort—"

"He bought a bus ticket. A coat on a rack works harder."

"Icky, please make the best of it. If I could get off work, I would."

"Fine, whatever." I pushed out of my seat.

I would think about it all night and then call an emergency Gum Chew meeting the next day.

"When will the lights be fixed?" I said as I left for my room.

My mom was full of shadows. Her hands wrung together on the table. "They'll be back tomorrow."

"Okay," I said, dragging out the word. "I need to call Grandpa." I had to understand why he wasn't coming.

Mom cleared her throat. "The phones will be back on in a day too."

"What's going on?"

"Nothing I can't fix. We have to wait for tomorrow's paycheck." She sighed. "All right, I better get to work. Big Herb will have a fit if I'm late again."

I flashed my teeth. Big Herb owns The Cravin' Shack diner where she works. Mom's boss is my archenemy. He's a despicable, belittling jerk. I want him to go down hard, but I can't. Not until my mom finishes night school and finds a job that deserves her.

Mom got up and kissed me. "It will be okay."

Sure. It will be okay, I think. *Because I'll make this all okay.*

CHAPTER 10

LIE

I blink away from the memory of the night before and turn to the sound of Tyler feverishly typing on his laptop. "You're unusually quiet," I say.

He raises a finger without looking up.

His brother leans back. "I know how bad you want this, man," Tyrone says to me, softening his voice. He directs a hand at Tyler. "But our mom won't let us go even if we get a chaperone. It's our auntie's birthday party that day." He scratches his head. "It sounds like your only choice is to see your dad. Your mom needs to work. I don't know. What would Sam Spade do?"

I stand straighter. My friends know my mentor well. I spew his lines and references at them all the time.

What would Sam Spade do? I close my eyes and watch him on my mental movie screen. "Sam Spade lets you see one thing . . . while his true plan unfolds without you knowing." Then I muse to myself, "Show what's expected while the plan unfolds . . ." I turn to Tyler, who is still typing on his computer. "All right, Tyler. I know that look. What have you found?"

"Your mom needs money, right?" he says.

"Right."

"Your dad already bought a ticket to . . . where does he live again?"

"Savannah."

"Give me a sec."

I snatch Tyrone's soda. Swirling a can is my signature comfort fidget. I pace. My thoughts twist with incomplete ideas. "Come on. We only have fifteen minutes left of lunch to crack this. I leave tomorrow." I swig the drink in my hand and gasp as warm; flat soda slithers down my throat. "Tyrone, this is bad."

Tyrone looks up from his cell phone. "That's not mine. It was here when we sat down."

After a stunned growl, I slam the can on the table and shove fresh gum in my mouth. I turn when Tyler calls out my name.

His fingers fly over the keyboard like he's the Beethoven of the Internet. The computer screen's glow reflects within his gleaming brown eyes. "What you said about Sam Spade gave me an idea."

"Go on."

"Your mom sees you off at the bus depot, which makes her happy. But what if you transferred buses at a stop and headed to the film festival?"

"By himself?" Tyrone's full attention is on his brother now. "He won't be able to get in."

"That's never stopped Ick before," Tyler adds with a grin. "Remember how he snuck into that PG-13 movie without a ticket after waiting for a big family to overwhelm the ticket taker?"

I nod along to Tyler. My eyes dash around the ground as I think through his words. "I can totally get in." I wave eagerly for him to carry on.

Tyler spins his computer around and pops his gum in his mouth. On the left side of his screen, he has set up a transfer ticket from Thomasberg depot, the first stop out of town. On the right side, a ticket to the 10th Annual Classic Film Festival is ready for checkout.

I make a sound like a Piccolo Pete firework is shooting out of my mouth. "You already did it?"

"Not quite," he says with a wince. "I need a credit card."

My heart sags like a three-day-old balloon. "I guess that's where this ends—"

A long arm reaches past me to Tyler. Enzo extends his parent's credit card.

"Enzo," I say. My frown meets his. "We can't use that. You'll get in so much trouble."

He wags his head. "Not if I say I lost it."

"But . . . you'll be coming with me."

"I'll stay home so no one will know." His soft voice hitches. "You need a great case."

A sting pricks my eyes. I suck in a breath. My best friend and I nod at each other.

Tyler quickly orders the tickets with Enzo's credit card. Tyrone is practically bouncing on his seat. He leans in and says, "You detour, nab the prize, and then head to your dad's."

All joy flutters. A new thought forms. A thousand dollars would be more than Mom would make this week. My sight becomes unfocused. I scratch at the invisible stubble on my chin. "If I win, I'm coming back home."

Tyrone's eyes grow wide. "And leave your dad waiting at the depot?"

"That will be a pretty big burn," Tyler says.

"It will." I stiffen my chin. A strained smirk pinches my cheek. The effort's heavy with the still-fresh memory of Dad's lie. Despite the din of cafeteria chatter, the silence of our group is thick.

Tyler clears his throat. "So that's the plan?"

"That's the plan," I reply.

"All right then. I better go print your tickets."

"I don't have a cell phone," I say. "I'm going into this blindly."

Tyrone snorts. "No way, man. We're not sending you out there alone." He flaps a brow at his brother. "Ty, I think this is the perfect occasion to try out *the mints*. Show him."

Tyler nods repeatedly. He digs in his big, black electronics bag. "It's a prototype. Ty and I have tested it." He pulls out a metal container.

My brows shoot up. "Altoids?" I say. "I'm a Gum Chew, not a Mint Muncher."

"Oh, these aren't your ordinary mints." His smile is wicked. "It's a satellite walkie-talkie."

CHAPTER 11

PODCAST

I roll through the plan for tomorrow until it feels comfortable. This could totally work. I will solve the mystery case at the film festival to win one thousand dollars for my mom and a Maltese Falcon trophy for myself. Maybe I'll even solve the case fast enough to have time to watch a classic movie or two. All while my mom thinks I'm on a bus to my dad. First things first, I need to get out of school.

The bell for the end of the day is still ringing. I'm already in the hallway heading toward the school exit. Kids race around me, bouncing with celebrations at the start of spring break. I wish finding joy was as easy as a ringing bell.

I ignore the snickers at how I dress and keep a swift pace. My focus is solely on preparing for tomorrow's adventure, but a detective never gets a break. I scan the halls, using just the dash of my eyes to sniff out my surroundings. A few kids stare at their phones. Nothing suspicious. The only crimes are selfie abuse and violence against fashion.

A doe-eyed boy snags my attention. He is pressed against a wall, hugging his books. Two larger boys fist their hands and chuckle as they move to the smaller kid. Without breaking my step, I grip the boy's shoulder and pull him with me.

"Kid," I whisper. "Tip: Never look lost in middle school." I hand him some Bubble-Yo gum from my pocket. "And always keep your head up . . . so you know what's coming." I point out the large boys watching us.

"Th . . . thanks," says the boy. He pops the gum in his mouth. "Say, you're that podcast kid, aren't you?"

A little smile breaks my scowl. "You are correct," I reply. I eye a girl checking out my handwritten podcast flyer hanging above a water fountain. "Now, get going. Remember, never stop paying attention." We split off at a fork. I take a few steps and pause before turning to the girl looking at my flyer. She sips water from the fountain.

The flyer says: *Want a smack of truth? Follow Gum Chew Nation.* It's signed with my name and a sketch of a bowtie.

My podcasts help me find new Gum Chews, and it gives me a place to share all I've learned about being a detective over the years.

"The Anatomy of a Proper Stakeout" has been the most successful of my podcasts, with ten subscribers. Each week, I review the basics of surveillance:

1. Stay invisible. Even in the open.

2. Don't blink. It's a practiced art. I can go for ten minutes. I usually wear sunglasses to protect my eyes from flies and dust.

3. Look busy. It pays to have a partner.

4. Tip your waitress. Otherwise, you put number one at risk.

In the most recent episode, I recounted my attempt to catch the Tooth Fairy with Enzo at age seven. The unsuccessful plot ended when Enzo passed out while he was supposed to be on watch. "Kids," I said, forcing my voice deep and serious. "Don't trust the Tooth Fairy. The cash is a distraction. Ask yourselves: What is this mysterious minx doing with all those teeth? Deliberate and I will follow up on next week's episode titled *I've Had My First Stakeout. Now What?*"

My other podcasts, "Interrogation and its Everyday Uses," "A Short Kid's Guide to the Universe," and "Worsted: A Fashion Opera," have yet to gain any followers other than Enzo.

There's one, "Hangry: Food to Soothe a Brooding Tween," only my mom follows. It's my grocery shopping wish list. "If you insist on bringing home rice cakes," I said in the last episode, "keep in mind they are simply rice puffed with air. The more air I take in, the more I let out. Consider at your own risk."

"You'll appreciate the truth," I say to the girl at the water fountain. My strained voice is in full force. She flinches and finishes her sip of water, but she doesn't run. Good sign. "See, my podcasts are catching wind. Kids want straight talk, not the fluff. I rip out the teddy bear innards for them and toss away the fur."

I grab the girl's limp hand and shake it. "Name's Icabum Plum." I cock a brow. "If you're looking for a sniff of roses, go fall in a garden. These aren't the podcasts for you. I'm the crow digging for worms. The fingerpicking for green gold. Tune in if you can handle it." I charge off, leaving the girl gaping. Toss another nickel in my subscriber jar. I caught a new one.

"Shoot!" I reach into the chest pocket of my jacket and pull out the voice recorder I always carry. It turns on with a *snick* sound. I press it close to my lips. "Tell my subscribers I'll be away for a while. I'm in search of a real Maltese Falcon."

CHAPTER 12

ESSAY

Billowing steam sulks around my morning shower like I'm on a foggy street in an old movie. It's Saturday, two hours until my bus takes off to my dad. I spent all night mowing over the details of today, and now if I think about it one more time, I might puke.

A new thought tugs at my growing dread. By the end of this week, I need a two-thousand-word essay in hand about what skills I think children should learn.

I blink at the tiled wall, letting a thought unfurl. The warm water shifts to arctic ice, and I shriek in a way I hope no one would ever hear.

"Mother!" I twist the shower knob. The hot water's gone. Mom must be washing dishes.

The icy water slaps my thoughts straight. An essay blooms in my head, moving forward like a steadfast cloud charged with lightning.

I toss out my detective tips like Tic-Tacs to morning breath. The skills I think kids should learn are the ones I live my life by. What if I recorded every tip I know?

I push through the lingering gloom circling the shower, wrapping a towel snugly around my hips. A jamboree of words to title my essay bob in my head. "The Laws of Unfair Happenings and How to Point Fingers."

"A Wolf in Wool: Memoirs of a Sleuthhound." "How to Bite First and Ask Questions Later." I wag my head at them all.

Maybe something about the tips. My jaw slacks. I blink furiously like I do when plans come together, and it paralyzes me.

"Move bonehead before it's gone."

I hurry to the voice recorder on the toilet seat and snatch it up. The recorder is always with me for stray thoughts worth keeping, mostly content for my podcasts. I lick my lips, hungry to speak, but I jump onto the stool and hastily scrub the mirror with my hand. I stare at myself, turn the recorder on, and press it close to my lips. With a cocked brow and holding a grimace, I say, "One Hundred Ways to be a Gum Chew with Gumption." A giggle relaxes my scowl and breaks me out of character. The title sounds even better out of my head.

Grandpa always says I have gumption, meaning a spirited resourcefulness. I frown, thinking about my grandpa again. I still haven't had a chance to find out what happened and why he couldn't come to take me to the festival.

I sink my face back into my hard-boiled, heavy-lidded look and continue with a tough-talk strain in my voice, "The Unofficial Guide for Unsanctioned Detectives Doing Unauthorized Work." I hurry and turn the recorder back on. "By the one and only Icabum Plum."

I've busted through my writer's block and keep going. The energy gives me goosebumps. Maybe I can knock out the introduction. I tap the recorder against my lips, freeze, and then turn it on. "Being a detective is a thankless job. But that's not the payment I look for. I keep the world safe, and in this self-help guide, you and others will too. This is everything you need to know to be a top-notch private eye. I've laid it all out like a picnic in July. But don't expect me to make the sandwich for you. You'll make your own sandwich. My tips will turn a moppet into a master. Listen to everything I say, and you too can—"

Thump, thump, thump. The bathroom door rattles under force. "Icky, who are you talking to?" Mom asks.

I turn off the recorder. "No one, Mom," I shout back at her through the door.

"Hurry out," she says. "I want time to settle you in at the bus depot before I have to be at work. And you need to eat breakfast. Pretzels don't count. Neither do M&Ms." I frown at her blatant disregard for the meal suggestion from my podcast.

"Be right out," I reply sweetly. I need to be careful not to spark suspicion.

I listen to the sound of her feet retreating down the hall and her sigh that carries with it. "Now, where was I? Dang. I lost my flow." Enough distraction. I need to get ready for today, but I'll keep the recorder close.

Water drips down my face as I lean my chin closer to the mirror. Not a beard hair. It's only a new freckle. My face is splattered with them like a mud spray from standing too close to a wet gutter on a busy street. Pity, it's not a hair. A five o'clock shadow would really suit my lifestyle. While examining my chin, I press the recorder to my lips again.

"Tip: Keep focus away from your words. Confusion rattles a culprit's lie. Hide your mouth and let your eyes do the talking. Boys, grow a beard and mumble. Girls, if a chin carpet's not for you, consider moving your lips less and talking through your teeth." Ninety-nine more tips to work out for my essay.

My shock of auburn hair lies limp when I lift from my slouch. A double palm of EZ GEL and a comb slick my hair back to a rock-hard shell just like the greats of the silver screen—it's what they used to call movie theaters in the old days. I lean forward again, thinking the light caught a hair I missed on my chin. I pick the piece of lint off with a scowl and turn my attention to my bare pectorals reflected in the medicine cabinet mirror. I flex and give up. Bones don't flex. I snatch the recorder briefly and add a tip.

"Tip: The size of the mind is stronger than the size of the body."

I flick open the medicine cabinet to get my Homme d'Blah cologne. It's French. A steal I found at Diamond Debby's Dollar Den. I lift a brow when the cabinet swings open. It's not the Homme d'Blah that's caught my attention. It's Mom's razor on the top shelf. My fingertips can barely reach it, but I pinch a hold of the pink razor and then lower back to my heels.

"Why do moms care about their legs being hairy when some of us have to worry about our faces?"

Maybe a shave will help the hair grow. I remember seeing Grandpa Gilbert shave once. He used water. I turn on the faucet, wet the razor, and drag it sideways across my chin. A half second later, I yowl as pain flares on my skin. The razor drops from my hand. Blood drips onto the white porcelain sink. A diluted red streak swirls into the drain. The Alfred Hitchcock moment makes me woozy. This isn't *Psycho,* the 1960 horror film that shamefully made me pee my trousers. This is real life. I catch a glimpse of my face as I stumble with shock off the stool: a nick in my chin and blood on my fingertips pressed against it.

My legs collapse beneath me like wet noodles. I thump down on my knees and crawl, leaving a bloody print trail. I reach for my recorder with feeble swats until I have it in my hand. I fall onto my back. My limbs are sprawled haphazardly.

The recorder rolls on. "Mom, if you're listening to this, I love you."

The bathroom door swings open. Mom's shriek makes my body jolt. Through squinted, weary eyes, I lift my head enough to see her. She sprints to the sink, soaks a rag, kneels at my side, and presses it to my face. I hiss.

"What in heavens are you doing, Icky?" she asks in a shrill voice.

"If . . . if I don't make it, I need you to know . . . I need you to know . . ." The stress of the day and the new pain are breaking me. I think the rest of what I wish I could say: *There's nothing Dad could have done that you haven't done for me. I owe everything to you.*

Mom slaps the side of my face twice.

I gasp. My emotions cork in my chest. Instead, I say, "I need you to know it was me who redirected the sprinklers. A real postman would deliver no matter what. Don't trust him."

"Get up," she says flatly.

My eyes snap open when she smacks my wound with a square of toilet paper to staunch the bleeding. "Clean this mess." Spoken like a true classic movie vixen: leave the victim to mop up his life. Mom sees the razor, grabs it, and brandishes it at me. "Not until you're eighteen." Fine. Who needs it? My beard will be incredible soon. I wince in pain. No more beard talk. Not when my chin is riddled with gashes.

A dozen quotes from my favorite Humphrey Bogart movies come to mind, but instead, I turn my pain into homework. I bring the recorder to my lips. It's still on. "Tip: Survival is your will to survive."

Mom spins around at the door. "What are you doing?" she asks.

I crack an eye open to see her. "My memoir," I lie. I can't have her attention on the essay. I need to fly under the radar.

"You're eleven," she replies. "What could you possibly have to say?"

"It's a cross between a cautionary tale and a self-help guide."

She snorts a laugh. "Where'd you get that anyway?" She points at the recorder.

"Dad left it behind when he found a new family." There's silence as Mom leaves the bathroom. I rest my head back on the floor with a frown. She hates it when I say that.

I drag the recorder back to my mouth. "Double Tip: Know when to shut up . . . And that truth hurts."

CHAPTER 13

MINTS

I hurry to my room after cleaning the scene in the bathroom. "Tip," I mumble into my recorder. "You are the mouse that knows how to get out of the maze."

"What's that?" Mom asks from a blind spot. She pins her name badge onto her waitress uniform.

I slam my back against the wall and keep my towel from dropping. "Huh?" My voice squeaks. I turn off the recorder. "Oh. I said you are a mom who knows how to get me out of a mess-zz."

Mom's brows crease. She glances at her watch. "We're leaving in twenty minutes."

I nod a dozen times as I scurry away. "Cool as flat soda. Calm down, Icabum. She'll only be suspicious about today if you act suspiciously."

"Wait," Mom calls out.

My body seizes.

"Tyler called," she adds. "He said something about the mints he gave you are bad. Enzo has more."

I fight my wince. Mints? The walkie! It worked fine last night. Tyler must be worried about something if he wants to change it. This day is already stumbling.

"That's why I stick to bubblegum," is my lame response to my mom. It comes out awkward, so I squint my eyes like I have a new thought as I back into my room.

After I close the door, I grin at the window across the room and rush to it. A pink sticky note with a sketch of a thumbs-up is stuck to the outside of the glass.

"Good work, Enzo."

I open the window, and my smile widens. A little white bag is sitting below my window on the gravel roof of a shed connected to the apartment building. I snatch my fishing pole and reel it up.

"Oh no," I whisper. The gravel's upheaved. Enzo's huge footprints are noticeable. "Tip," I say to the recorder. "A footprint at a scene can mean more or less than it seems. It's what's happening around the print to give it purpose." I might as well write my essay as I live it.

I know I don't have the time, but I use the fishing pole to compromise the evidence, dragging it through the prints to level the surface. Satisfied, I close the window.

At my desk, I push miscellaneous research out of the way and rip open the bag to examine the new walkie-talkie. The antenna pulls out clean from the side. The lid flips up, revealing a microphone on the bottom and a speaker on the top. There's a dial for volume, lights for power level, and a button to talk. It doesn't look different than the other walkie, but if Tyler deems the other is bad, it's for a good reason. I push the talk button and whistle a birdcall. No response.

"Come on," I whisper.

I sit the walkie on my desk and stare at my empty *Board of Missing* while I wait. Photos and notes about lost items are usually posted on this board, but work has been slow these days. I finger through an old pile of files on my desk and freeze at the green construction paper folder before pulling my hand away quickly. I still haven't been able to throw away the *Dad* case.

I click on the recorder. "Tip: Some cases are never solved." Never truly solved, that is.

My foot bounces. I don't feel an ounce of regret for switching today's plans and ditching my dad. Some things in my life are more important.

No matter how much fun the film festival is today, I can't lose focus on the prize. I've read everything I could find about the 10th Annual Classic Film Festival. Its featured case is kept a secret. All I know is that I need to be there by 1:00 p.m. If I don't get there by then, this day is a bust.

It's an easy plan. Get in, crack the case, win the Maltese Falcon trophy and money, and get out. Mom is the one I worry about most. I hate disappointing her, but if I play this just right, we'll be a thousand dollars richer, and it will soften any grounding I may earn.

I flick my silver pocket watch open and closed. It belonged to Grandpa Gilbert. He gave me the watch for my tenth birthday when I changed my name. I wear it and polish it every day. I still haven't been able to reach my grandpa. What's going on with him? I clutch the watch. At least he'll be with me in spirit today.

I don't care that kids laugh at me because I dress differently. As the saying goes, *being like everybody is the same as being nobody.*

"Tip: No matter how included you feel," I tell my recorder, "be different. It's how you see the differences in others."

I whistle into the walkie again. Bird whistles sing through the speakers a beat later.

"Why the new walkie?" I whisper. "Wait. Don't answer. My mom might hear. Tyler and Tyrone, stay on alert. I have a contest to win. I'll need your help. Over."

A voice enters the speaker like a bird that can talk. "Cheeeat-errr," one of the Chokeberrys says. Most likely Tyrone. I roll my eyes.

"You'll be singing another tune when I don't do your math homework. Over." Instead of cash, I pay the Chokeberrys with A's on homework for their help on special projects. It's costing me a week of their math homework to get the walkie-talkie support team and a fake seventh-grade Don Kiwi Middle School ID. The ID and an altered consent form say that I'm twelve, so I can jump on the train back home with the prize money in hand.

Tyrone chirps back in. "Brrooo-ken Waaal-kie—"

"Clam it, stay tuned, and talk soon. Over and out." I frown at the Altoids case before I close it. One of the five power bars is gone. This satellite walkie can go as far as two hundred miles, but what good is that if the battery is dead? I slam down the antenna and get to work on dressing for my big day.

I raise the recorder to my lips while I yank out my pre-packed bags from my closet: a leather satchel and a garment bag.

"Tip: Beware ennui. Ennui is boredom from a lack of interest, and it will hinder motivation. A threat all ages can fall victim to." I'm going to prevent ennui during this spring break, even if just for one afternoon.

I toss the satchel and garment bag onto my bed. I have to be cautious of what I wear right now. I decide on my dark gray three-piece suit and black bowtie. Anything too smart and Mom will get suspicious. Mom's a wreck about sending me on the bus alone. Any little thing out of the norm may set her off and blow this whole operation.

A bowtie is my signature and a staple for a casual outing. My favorite wide-brimmed fedora hat, the same design Sam Spade wore, is on me every time I leave the house. Mom would notice nothing out of the ordinary compared to other moms seeing their children in sweats and baseball caps. I'll never wear those two things again in my life.

The jacket shrugs on tight. The trousers are slim and tailored. My argyle socks are bright and playful. My black Oxfords are polished. "Tip: See the moon in the shine of your shoes. Your style is a tool . . . and the shine could be used as a spy mirror." I can tell a lot about a person by the shine of their shoes.

My fedora hat slips on my head and down over one of my brows. Grandpa Gilbert's pocket watch is linked to my waistcoat button and rests in its pocket. My eyes are a bit puffy from being up all night worrying about today. Hopefully, Mom doesn't read into it. I give myself an impressed frown and a nod to the mirror. Almost perfect, except for the bloody toilet paper square stuck to my chin, which now looks kind of cool.

My Bogart frown sags. Mom doesn't know I read Dad's text to her this morning.

CHAPTER 14

HEAD ON

*T*ell *Junior to dress normal,* Dad wrote in his text to my mom.

I try to ignore it, but his words keep finding their way back into my thoughts.

"This is normal, Dad," I say. "I'm no longer that kid who changed for you. I'm not Junior anymore. I'm Icabum now."

I look in the mirror. My eyes flicker with purpose as I lift the recorder to my mouth. "Tip: Dress the part despite what anyone says. There's no such thing as overdressed. Just watch Sam Spade. Plain dress shirt, plain tie, plain jacket. A no-effort combo but always great," I say, finding my groove. My comfort clicks into place like it does every time I talk about fashion. My "Worsted: A Fashion Opera" podcast episodes can go on for hours sometimes. "Tailor your wear, and it will tailor your life—it's the key to *confidence.* And it doesn't hurt to look flashy exiting the locker you've been shoved into."

"Head on straight today, Icabum," I add to myself as I straighten my bowtie. My nerves tumble, and I distract myself with the recorder again. "Tip: Keep a steady moral compass. Right is still right. Wrong is still wrong." This tip is a stretch for me today.

I leave the recorder running and chew on the inside of my mouth. "Tip: Detectives live in the gray of life, just as the sun is to light and shadows are to darkness."

I pull out the contents of my satchel one more time and lay them on my bed: film festival ticket, bus transfer ticket to Old Town, recorder, field notebooks, lock picks, walkie-talkie, Bubble-Yo gum, and wallet with $63 from my savings. I consider my pack of zip ties for citizen arrests and opt to take just one. I pick up the two tickets.

"Let's do this," I say.

My doorknob squeaks as it turns. I shove the tickets under my pillow before making myself look busy repacking my things in my bag.

"Breakfast is on the table, Icky," Mom says as she cracks open the door. She can't open it very far. I make it so only I can slip in. My stacks of cataloged field notebooks, full of my old reports of strange occurrences and unusual happenings around town, litter the floor. It's a barrier so Mom doesn't venture too far into my room and snoop around in my investigations. She wouldn't be pleased with how far I sometimes go to solve a case—sewer crawls, trunk stakeouts, and the girls' locker room wearing a wig. The last one helped me nab a prevalent ring of counterfeit scrunchies.

I release a slow breath and then turn with a smile. "Be right there."

She doesn't leave. Instead, her eyes well up with tears.

I sigh. "I'm going to be fine, Mom."

Her lower lip quivers when she nods. "Open the door, and let me help you pack."

"No!" I clear my throat and lower my voice. "No. I got it. Here, take my garment bag." I hand the bag to her and make haste to throw my things in the satchel.

"Tyler's mints?" she says as I reach for the walkie.

My heart stops. "Tyler thinks all my gum chewing is keeping me short."

Mom laughs. "Come on."

I back out of the room, bags in hand, searching to make sure I haven't left out anything incriminating about today's deception.

I catch myself in the mirror one last time. Easy. What could go wrong? I rattle my head with a stumble. Like Sam Spade would, I have to expect everything will go wrong.

CHAPTER 15

GRANDPA

I attack my plate of food with harried speed. Ham and eggs are all I eat for breakfast since I read that it was Humphrey Bogart's favorite. "If it was good enough for the man who played Sam Spade, it's good enough for me," I said in a Hangry podcast episode to Mom. Right now, I'm too distracted even to taste my breakfast. My schedule tumbles over and over again in my head, so every move I make today feels as simple as breathing.

Mom is talking in her *this is important* voice, and I am nodding as if I understand that it is important.

"You'll be on bus #32 the whole way to Savannah. Four and a half hours. It stops three times for fifteen minutes before you reach your dad around 1:30 p.m.: Thomasberg, Steelville, and Haywood," Mom says, or something like that. I'm not entirely listening. "Make sure you use the restroom each time," she tacks on. How much water does she think I drink?

Her words settle on me like sticky subway air, but I focus on *my* schedule.

One hour to Thomasberg. Fifteen minutes to transfer to bus #55 before it takes off at 10:20 a.m. to Old Town where the film festival is. One-and-a-half-hour ride. The contest starts at 1:00 p.m. Destroy the competition. Collect my winnings. If time allows, find a movie. A train leaves from Old Town to Circle's End at 5:00 p.m.

"I want you to use the ladies' restroom. You're small, so you can get away with it, and I've written you a note," Mom continues. I flash her narrowed eyes. She shows me the letter that reads *I give my son permission to be in here–Freyda Plum* before she folds it up and slips it into my jacket.

I scowl at her for both the comment about being small and suggesting I use the ladies' restroom, and then I go back to eating and thinking. The fifteen minutes at the first stop in Thomasberg is crucial. I can't miss my transfer bus.

"Be friendly," Mom adds. "But if anyone makes you feel uncomfortable, it's okay to be rude."

My brow lifts at that. I nod. Solid advice, Mom. Editing that for my essay as a tip. Detectives can be rude.

"I feel sick," she moans and checks her watch. Her pinched-worried-mom-face is crumbling into catastrophic panic. "I've called the bus depot several times to make sure they are aware of who you are and that you're on your own. There are some bus delays today, but they don't affect the Express fleet you are on. Oh, when I went by to see the depot manager, he asked me to have you wear this button, so they know who you are."

And here it is. I knew Mom would do something like tape me to the seat or cover me in bells. I groan. "Is this necessary?" I snatch the button. "Oh, no way!" I add when I examine it. "Nuh-uh. Not going to do it." The button is yellow with a toddler drawing of a white bus and a bold black print that reads *VROOM VROOM.*

"Wear it," she says sternly and lets out a content sigh when I comply. "And if for any reason you are lost or left behind, call me right away and stay where you are."

I make a show of dragging my recorder to my lips. "Tip: You are never lost if you know where you're headed."

Mom's laugh doesn't reach her eyes. I take a big bite of eggs and mumble to her with my mouth full. "How do I call you? I don't have a cell phone. Remember?"

I hate myself for the worry line I add between her brows. "The depot clerks will let you use their phones."

She lets out a long breath and glances at what I'm wearing. My chin stiffens, bracing for her to tell me what my dad said in his text. Her eyes soften as she says, "You look handsome, sweetheart."

I smirk and pat her hand to soothe her worry.

"Did you bring a swimsuit?" she asks.

"My trousers are a poly-blend. They'll be okay around water."

Mom snorts a laugh and tugs on the rim of my hat. "And did you get your toothbrush? Chewing gum is not the same as brushing."

I wince.

"Go get it." She flicks my hat.

I peel off my chair with my recorder to my mouth. "Tip: A good smile is the best kind of weapon."

The house phone rings when I reach the doorway. I tuck behind the wall to listen in case the call has anything to do with today.

"Hey, Mom," I hear and stand up straighter. Grandma Ginger! I can find out what's up with Grandpa. I freeze when I hear my mom's voice quaver when she asks, "How's Papa feeling? What did the doctor say?"

"Grandpa Gilbert is . . . sick?" I whisper.

I creep back to the door.

Mom sniffs. "No, I haven't told him."

A numbness pours over my head and into every bone, freezing me where I stand.

There's a pause. Mom jolts as she peeks around the corner, surely having heard my heavy breathing.

"Let me call you back," she says into the phone before she hurries to end the call. A tear breaks free as she pulls the phone away. "Icky," she says, voice hoarse. Her eyes are wide and red-rimmed. She doesn't say anything else as she stares at me standing there.

My lips flap and words come out, but it doesn't feel like they are working together when I say, "Grandpa's sick." Not a question. More an admission of what Mom is unable to speak.

She nods. "That's why he couldn't drive up. Send your love and good thoughts to him."

My face scrunches. The news threatens to snap the weight already on my shoulders and bring me to my knees. The second most important person in my life is sick. I haven't moved when Mom repeats my name.

My eyes slowly blink as I gather my wits. I lift them.

She releases her lips from between her teeth. "Why don't you call him from Dad's when you get there?"

I force myself to nod. My mom and grandpa need me. Today, I swear above everything to come through for them. I'm getting my Maltese Falcon. After that, I'm taking the train to see Grandpa Gilbert.

CHAPTER 16

DOOM DOOM

The bus depot bustles with people trying to get out of this boring town for the weekend. Mom gives me side eyes. She's turned from fretted Freyda to wary, and I fear my guard may have slipped in my worrying about my grandpa. She knows my impulsive history. My record is about as clean as a mirror in front of a curious toddler.

I try to shift her suspicion and layer on the pre-teen moping. I stretch my face with plain boredom and a hint of irritation. The bloody toilet paper is off my chin, but the cut's ache still lingers, adding to my grumpiness.

"I don't want to go," I mumble, keeping my muscles loose. Otherwise, she'll read too much into my distraction. She would be curious if I didn't put up a little fight until the very end, and I can't look too eager to go.

Mom pulls our car into a spot near a row of bullet-shaped buses. White smoke puffs out their back ends like chilly farts. She chews on her lip. "Icky, don't do this." Her eyes puddle with tears. It worked, and it only made me feel terrible. "Your dad asked for you to come."

I brush off her incessant lie and roll my eyes. "Is he tired of being a lying, dead-beat dad?"

"He's not—"

"You've covered for him long enough." I've gone too far, but my dad has a way of sharpening my edge.

Mom turns off our rickety car. It stutters and finally chokes into silence. "Icky." She takes a deep breath.

I drag my eyes slowly to her. "What?" they imply.

"Show him who you are," she says.

Show him who I am? Fine. I'm someone who takes care of my family. I nod when her gaze lingers on me.

"You will see your friends again soon," she adds with a hand brushing my cheek.

I jerk the door open, itching to look at my pocket watch. If I'm late, this is all ruined. She snags my hand. "Be careful, not careless."

I allow myself to smile and say, "An excellent tip." I take her in for a moment and remember what today is all about.

"You've taught me well," she replies with a wink. All suspicion fizzles away with her smile. Good. She won't be holding that smile at the end of today when she hears what I've done, where I've gone, and where I'm going.

After Mom hugs me for a humiliating length of time and recites my schedule like a nursery rhyme, I swat away her lingering smooch. A tear streaks down Mom's blushed cheek as she straightens my stupid *VROOM VROOM* button, and then she leaves me on a bench where I wait to board bus #32.

Mom would have stayed with me the whole time if not for her boss, Big Herb. One day, I will take him down, but right now, I have to focus.

Dozens of people cluster under the awning to wait for their buses. Whenever I'm in a new place, I scan the folks around me. Vigilance is a word for keeping careful watch for danger, and the skill needs conditioning. I oil my vigilance like a leather belt. I jot down in my field notebook: *Tip: Strengthen your memory.* My expertise as a detective depends on my ability to remember everything.

Last summer, after an all-night, caffeine-fused detective movie binge, I got an idea for a memory training system. I call it E.H.S., which stands for eyes, hand movement, and speed. Grouping these three things can tell me a lot about someone. It also gives my memory a foundation to remember if I need to follow up with an officer. I shift in my seat, look around, and switch into training mode.

The woman across from me: Her blue eyes are narrowed but distant. Her arms are crossed over her chest. Angry, annoyed? At whom, what? She glances at the clock. Her bus must be late.

I stifle a yawn but halt midway. A girl about my age sitting with her dad watches me. My face flushes. She has brunette curls pulled back with a white ribbon and milk chocolate eyes that . . . are staring at my button. I pinch my eyelids tight and rip the stupid thing off my coat. An idea forms. I pull out my black evidence marker, write on the button, and pin it back on. The girl giggles at my button, which now says *DOOM DOOM* instead of *VROOM VROOM.*

Back to work. I pat the pocket in my coat where Mom put my bus ticket. My body flares with panic until I remember I moved it to my pant pocket. I let out a long breath.

"Relax, Icabum. You have your ticket—" I jolt forward and shout, "Tickets!"

CHAPTER 17

BuS #32

My heart races. I can't catch my breath. Tickets! My bus transfer ticket and film festival ticket. I left them under my pillow. The air is thinning. My face burns. I rip the Altoids box from my bag and flip the lid open.

"Mayday! Mayday!" I whisper intensely into the box. A few people standing nearby look my way. I cover my face and the walkie with the flap of my coat.

The Gum Chews chime in right away. I don't care to consider who's who.

"Here, Ick!"

"Here."

"What's up?"

"Emergency," I say. "I left my bus transfer ticket and the film festival ticket under the pillow on my bed. Over."

A string of creative curse words replies. "Ick, it's Tyler. I'll tap into the depot communications and hold up your transfer as long as I can."

"Budget Hound fleet bus #55 at 10:20 a.m." Now, how to get the tickets? Enzo has a key to my house—

"On it," Enzo replies in his low monotone voice. My buddy never hesitates if I'm in trouble.

"Can you bring it to Thomasberg depot? 10:00 a.m. Be careful. I don't want you connected to today's ruse." Oh no! Enzo canceled his credit card. He can't take a taxi.

There's a pause. Enzo returns. "Artie said he'll help me get your inhaler and bring it to you."

Artie is the Lemon family's driver. I let out a breathless laugh. "Right. Inhaler. Good thinking, buddy." I'm asking a lot of him right now, but I have no other choice. "Thanks, guys. Over and out."

I remove my coat flap from over my face and settle into my slouch with my garment bag on my lap and the leather satchel slung across my chest. I knock the back of my head against the wall behind me enough times to calm myself.

"Hello!" chirps a woman as she shuffles over to me. She sits down inside my personal space barrier. "First time on a bus—" Her radioactive smile falls like an atomic bomb when she sees my button. She clears her throat. "What a brave boy all on your own."

The woman gets one of my side-eye specials. "I'm not on my own." I never tell a stranger I'm on my own. Instead, like Sam Spade, I carry the confidence like an army is behind me.

"Oh." The woman giggles. "I'm headed on bus #32, so I guess you got me too!"

I take the woman in, long and hard, until she shifts to give me space. "I never told you I was on bus #32."

The woman swats a playful hand. "I guessed since we're near the bus." She pauses and looks at me closely. "Everything okay?"

"Peachy," I mumble. I shift my bags to create a smooth transition as I turn my back on the woman. Like Mom said, if someone makes you feel uncomfortable, it's okay to be rude. I check my pocket watch. It's 9:00 a.m. on the dot. We should be boarding already, but the bus driver slowly strolls down the ramp toward bus #32. I jump to my feet and charge toward him.

"Ready to board," I say upon approach.

The beady-eyed man scowls down at me and slowly sips the steaming cup of coffee in his hand. His appraisal takes too long. I adjust the garment bag in my arms, push the rim of my hat up a tad, and raise a brow to appraise him back. The bus driver looks like a bodybuilder crammed into a Boy Scout uniform, as harmonious as the devil at a tea party. His nametag reads *Vito*.

"I'll need you to sit up front," Vito says with a condescending tilt of his head.

"My ticket lets me sit where I please," I reply, weighing him. I remind myself to note a tip for my essay. *Be self-confident, not overconfident.* This guy has bad news written all over him, like a gossip blog on a Sunday morning. No one needs to be that strong to drive a bus. I'll keep my distance.

Vito looks past me at the personal space violator at my back. She squeals in my ear, "Are you excited?"

"Sure," I grumble when my hearing recovers. "Buses remind me of big coffins." I don't look back, but it quiets her.

I board the bus, keeping my baggage close. Vito watches me, ignoring the greetings of the other passengers.

I pause halfway down the bus and choose a seat on the right side with a clear view of the driver when he takes the wheel. Vito catches my eye in the window. I turn from the heat and busy myself with my bags and recorder.

"Tip: Deadpan cynicism. Let it be your filter—"

"What's that, dear?" My middle-aged shadow backs her caboose onto my seat and blocks me in, cramming me against the wall.

Oh, for the love of . . . I turn off my recorder. "Ma'am," I say, fighting my bite and replacing it with sticky honey, "would you mind sitting next to the window? I have this rash on my left side, and it itches constantly. My elbow will keep getting in your way."

The woman tightens her lips in a restrained grimace. "How about I just give you your space?"

"Lovely," I say sweetly. "Tip," I whisper as she moves away. "Be like a snake charmer. Get them to do what you want." Speaking of snakes, I glance at Vito watching me. His eyes drift to the crazy woman flopping down with a loud grunt on the bench behind me. I itch my armpit every time someone else considers sitting with me.

Outside, the luggage compartment slams shut. Vito loads himself last. He takes his throne at the wheel and mumbles "Thomasberg" into the mic. He adjusts his mirror until I can see myself in it. I slump low.

With one hour to Thomasberg, I try to distract myself from Enzo and the forgotten tickets. I pull out my field notebook while I scan the people on the bus. The recorder will draw too much attention. I have an essay to write, but it's important to read what's happening around me.

Tip, I write. *Sight is an infinite amount of details, not just one picture. Wade through it like a sandy beach to find what is out of place.*

The bus rumbles and jolts me against the seat as it rolls one step closer to my destiny. . . or doom, depending on what transpires at the Thomasberg depot. I unwrap a Bubble-Yo and pop it in my mouth. Gnawing on my gum forces my mouth into a tough-guy grimace, the uniform for Gum Chews.

Tip, I write with a yawn. *Allow time to think.* I tap my lip. The rumbling of the bus loosens my joints. I slouch further into my seat. *Tip: Do your research.* I blink to clear my sight. *Tip: Constant reasoning and thinking allow little time for sleep. If you stay ahead, you can sleep later—* My hand slides slowly off the page. My body follows it to the window. Despite the excitement and the risk of being alone, staying up late last night pays its due to the Sandman. I fall asleep.

CHAPTER 18

STRIKE

I jolt awake when the bus screeches and judders to a stop. Vito mumbles into the microphone, and it sounds like he says, "Thomasberg."

"What!" I glance to my side and jolt again. The woman who had sat behind me is now sitting beside me.

"First stop," she chirps. Her puff of brown hair waddles where it's trapped above her sun visor. She leans in like she has a secret. "You should use the restroom before we take off again."

I blink at her. "I thought you were sitting behind me." My tongue is tacky from falling asleep with gum in my mouth.

"I kept you from falling over!"

I push harder against the side of the bus, check my pocket for my wallet, and glance around. Travelers file out of the bus. Through the shuffle, Vito watches me from his seat. I break my stare to look at my watch—10:15 a.m., we're fifteen minutes behind! I have five minutes to find Enzo and get on the bus to Old Town.

"You know what?" I say to the crazy lady, a little too rushed to sound natural. "I do have to pee. If you'll excuse me." I fumble to my feet and pause as the woman shifts to let me pass instead of getting up. My lip snarl is checked before she can see it. I gather my things and decide to give her the toots view as I shuffle my way, trying not to touch her.

A few feet before I get to the driver's seat, Vito stands up with a broad-chested stretch and looks down at me. "Be back in fifteen minutes," he says. "I don't want to have to go looking for you." He pops a knuckle.

I narrow my eyes at him. Vito is a little too curious about me. We hold a stare until he decides to walk down the bus's steps in front of me. I hiss to myself.

Off the bus, I scan the depot. Five minutes until bus #55 is scheduled to leave. Who knows how long Tyler can hold the bus? I need to find Enzo, but now I have Vito in front of me.

My stomach tumbles when I don't see my best friend right away. The depot is crowded, but many people are in uniforms, holding signs and chanting.

A protest.

"Budget Hound unfair!" cries out a woman.

"Fair wages now!" yells a man.

There are too many people moving around. I can't see. I'm counting on Enzo not to mess this up, but the likelihood of that happening is as strong as a cup of joe. He's reliable and the best partner I could ask for, but sometimes, he gets confused. I'm late. What if he left? Or maybe he just went to the restroom? My back stiffens. That's precisely where Vito is heading.

I continue to scan the depot while I track Vito. My shoes click on the cement. Vito glances to the side. He feels me tailing him.

"Tip: Feathered feet," I whisper to my recorder. An elephant would make a good detective, said no one ever. Thirty feet to the restroom, twenty-five, twenty, fifteen.

Vito halts when a giant shadow appears in the doorway to the restroom. He steps aside to let the man pass, glancing back at me before entering. The man that leaves is much taller than Vito and no man at all. It's Enzo. My muscles tense to keep from sprinting to him.

His jet-black hair gleams. Enzo's usual shy, doe-eyed stare shifts nervously. He's worried for me, I'm sure, but I also know that new places and crowds make him uneasy. He's frozen in place as busy travelers scurry around him. He zips up the neck of his favorite tracksuit, shoves his hands in his pockets, and lifts his shoulders to his ears with his eyes pinched tight. Oh no! I need to get to him fast.

My heart races as I throw a sharp bird whistle through the crowd. Enzo's eyes find me in a blink. His mouth opens with a gasp. I nod my head to a nearby bench. He reaches it first and sits at the far edge. Enzo knows the rules of a five-fingered exchange, as well as he knows interrogations, stakeouts, and fingerprinting. Sitting down on the opposite side of the bench from him, I scan the crowd, ready to tap my finger for the exchange, but I flash my teeth instead.

"Did you go potty, dear?" The crazy lady from the bus shuffles over to me. A gleam in her eye tells me she is looking to sit between Enzo and me.

I lean forward over my luggage. "I'm a little gassy. I like letting it all out before inconveniencing anyone in tight spaces." I hear Enzo snicker.

The crazy lady controls her grimace like she did before and redirects herself to another bench. While she's distracted trying to sit, I tap my finger on the bench, and Enzo slides the tightly folded tickets to me under his hand. We've practiced this move a thousand times to pass notes in class. The exchange is lost to the naked eye.

"Good job, buddy," I whisper. "You best be going. Stay safe, and I'll see you in a week."

"A week? But you're going to win and come home." His whisper is a mouse squeak, but I always hear him.

"I will win, but . . ." I can't fight the strain on my face. "Grandpa Gilbert is sick."

At that, Enzo sits up. He always travels with my mom and me to my grandparents' house in Florida. I hate the worry and sadness that flares in his eyes.

"I can't explain now," I add, eyeing the crazy lady. "I have to be there for him. I wish you could go."

"I'll miss you," replies my friend with a frown.

"I'll miss you too," I reply. Enzo and I need each other like ham and eggs, mac and cheese, leather gloves and winter. But today, I'm on my own. "Gotta split. I'm late . . . and I think I'm being followed." The crazy lady waves at me.

Enzo squints his green eyes into the sun. A sad smirk grows as he peels away his jacket before leaving the bench. I chuckle at his abandoned jacket.

"You're a master Gum Chew, Enzo."

CHAPTER 19

ICKY WICKY

I snatch the jacket and rush to Bargain Hound bus #55. The giant-size hooded jacket reaches my knees when I throw it on. I fumble with my garment bag as I do. Vito is now outside the restroom, scanning the Thomasberg depot. I spin my body around a group of protesters and head in the opposite direction of him. The large digital clock on the wall reads 10:26 a.m.

"Come through for me, Tyler," I say.

I sprint along the rows of buses and slide to bus #55. It's empty, but a young attendant stands out front. I throw the jacket's hood over my hat.

"Oh, hello," she says. "You must be DJ Icky Wicky. Your manager called." She clears her throat. "You look a lot younger than I expected."

I bob my head a few times. Tyrone. He calls me Icky Wicky all the time. I hate it so much.

She shrugs. "Okay, follow me. We'll get you to your show as fast as we can."

I glance over my shoulder and catch Vito scanning buses. "Where are we going?" I ask, keeping my voice low.

"You didn't hear? Bargain Hound is on strike. But don't worry, you've been rerouted."

She leads me toward another bus, heading back in the direction I came from. I pull my hat and hood as far down over my face as I can and hide among a group of people while I pass Vito.

The driver of the new bus is tagged *Wanda*. She turns with a scowl as I brandish my crumpled ticket at her.

Wanda takes it and evaluates it too long. "You've made us late, kid," she says with a raspy voice. "Consent form."

I rip out my wallet, flashing her my fake middle school ID, and unfold an altered version of Mom's bus consent form.

"In you go," Wanda says.

I leap up the bus's steps and breathlessly slouch in a seat. I glance out the window and see the crazy lady from bus #32 searching the hedges. She stops to talk with Vito. Something is definitely up with those two.

"Vroom, Vroom. Doom, Doom," I say as the bus rumbles. With my hat brim lowered over my eyes, I hide until we are out of the depot, grinning uncontrollably.

"Honey," says a man on a cell phone behind me. "I won't be in Old Town until two o'clock. Bargain Hound drivers are on strike. I'm being rerouted."

I snap upright. "Wanda!" I cry out. Everyone on the bus looks at me. "This bus won't get to Old Town until two o'clock?" I'm breathing heavily. My ticket said I would arrive by noon. Now I'll miss the contest. I need to be there no later than 1:00 p.m.

Wanda nods. "Three stops between. Seems I'm the only one working these days." The last part she grumbles to herself.

I press against the window and watch Vito, the crazy lady, and the Thomasberg depot disappear. Enzo and his driver are long gone.

CHAPTER 20

WANDA

After I feel like my head will spin off my neck, I move to the seat behind Wanda and riddle her with questions.

"Yes," she says. "For the tenth time, kid, we'll arrive at Old Town by two o'clock. Get behind the line."

I step back into my seat. "I can't. I have to be there no later than one o'clock." This is terrible. I'm already off course. Maybe I go straight to my grandparents and forget all this. No! This is my great case. I have to get to the film festival by one o'clock.

"Your mom didn't check on your ticket before you arrived?" Wanda says.

I better heel before she tightens the screw. "My mom's a little near-sighted," I reply. Wanda's brows furrow. "When's the next stop? I will ... uh ... have her call in a ride."

"Next stop is at 11:30 a.m. in Bear Bottom."

Okay, okay. I hurry to the empty back of the bus and dig in my bag for my walkie. "Mayday, mayday, mayday! Over," I whisper into it for the second emergency of the day. It's not even noon yet.

A beat later, I hear, "Yo, we're here!" Tyrone Chokeberry says, out of breath. "What's up, DJ Icky Wicky? Over."

I growl at the name. "My transfer bus is being rerouted. I'm on Highway 6 to Bear Bottom. Tell me how far Bear Bottom is from Old Town. Over."

"Ty's on it! Uhh . . . uhh . . . okay, okay. Bear Bottom . . . an hour and a half away from Old Town. Over."

I snarl at the roof of the bus. That puts me at the film festival just in time for the contest, if I'm lucky to find it right away. "I'm going to find another way to the festival from there. Stay tuned. Over."

"Whoa. Wait, Ick. If you're thinking of getting off the bus at Bear Bottom, don't. Over."

"What? Why? I have to. I won't get to Old Town until two o'clock on this bus. From Bear Bottom, I'm closer to getting there in time. I *need* to be in that contest. Over."

"Ick, it's Tyler. Bear Bottom is no good, man. Don't stop there. Repeat. Don't stop there. The reviews say there are a lot of thieves, and most of the town is homeless. Over."

"My decision is already made." I watch a power bar on the walkie blink out. I only have two bars left. "Tyler. The battery on this walkie is horrible. Over," I say, ignoring all his fussing.

"Plug in the charger! Over."

"What charger? Over."

"I gave it to Enzo. That's why I sent a new chargeable walkie. Over."

"Oh," chimes in Enzo's deeper mumble. "Yeah. I have it . . . um, over."

I press the heel of my hand into my eye. "If you don't hear from me by one o'clock," I say, "call in the cavalry. Over and out."

CHAPTER 21

BEAR BOTTOM

An hour later, at Bear Bottom depot, I jump off the bus the moment the door hisses open. Not one person follows me off. The stench hits first like a jumbo fart blast after an all-you-can-eat bean buffet. Bear Bottom isn't the type of seedy where plants grow. It's a town that hugs to the shadows, and people stare furtively through their tangled mini blinds. The silent hum of sleepless nights and abandoned days unsettles my stomach. The air squishes against my skin like soggy bread. If I tossed a dime here, it'd never hit the ground. Tyler was right. It's bad news.

I hold my luggage tight and sprint to the ticket clerk. There are no other buses at this small depot. A few people are scattered around, but they all appear to live here.

"I need to get to Old Town," I say to the bored-looking clerk with his feet kicked up on the counter.

He points at the bus I just left. An effort that appears to exhaust him.

"No, I need to get there faster."

"There's nothing," the man says. "Sorry, kid." Wanda honks the bus's horn at me.

"Are you sure?" I try to keep my voice steady, but it still pitches. "I have to get there by one o'clock."

The man shakes his head. I eye the thick bars and tangled barbwire that cage in the ticket booth.

"And the depot closes in two hours," the man adds.

I stiffen my chin as a sob scratches my throat. I stagger away from the booth into an open square and turn on my recorder. "Tip: Control your emotions. Cry on the inside."

"You lookin' to go to Old Town?" asks an aged familiar-sounding voice. I turn quickly and squint into the light surrounding the figure walking toward me. The voice. The slouched walk. The driving cap. My heart flutters. It can't be.

"Grandpa?" I say.

The man even chuckles like my grandpa. "I'm someone's grandpa, kid," he says. "Not yours." Light fills his face, and I blink the illusion away. I still see an older gentleman, but he's not my grandpa. His dirty boots look like they've been worn through a decade or two. He stares down at me with tired eyes the color of golden sunlight. His brown hair is frosted white above the ears and tucked beneath a weathered driving cap. The man's vest and trousers might have been nice once, but their well-worn fit sits loose over a wrinkled, oversized dress shirt.

"Sorry, I . . . you look like my grandpa," I say.

"Is he supposed to meet you here?" he replies.

I caution against revealing too much info. "I need to go to Old Town."

"I can get you there," the man says, slipping his hands into his pockets.

Everything I pride myself on about being safe and vigilant is blaring with a warning until he adds, "I'm a taxi driver," and points to his cab.

I take a tentative step forward. "I'd like to see your license."

The man chuckles. It's so much like my grandpa's laugh that it eases the tension in my shoulders. He reaches into his back pocket and flings open his wallet to show his license. "Name's Ben," he says. The name checks out. "Why are you out here alone, kid? You're dressed a little too nice for the likes of Bear Bottom. Mismatching, but nice." I'm still wearing Enzo's jacket. I'd take it off now, but the air might stain my suit.

Again, I don't give him more than necessary. "I need to get to Old Town quickly. What will it cost?" I only have $63, but most of it is for my train ticket.

"Why do you want to go to Old Town?" he asks.

Too many questions. "I've got somewhere I need to be," I answer.

"I see." Ben cocks his head. His unique eyes catch the afternoon light. "What are you, like, ten years old?"

Rude. I stand up straighter. "Twelve," I lie. I don't flash my fake Middle School ID and let him know where I live.

"And where's your mom and dad?"

"Expecting me," I lie again. I don't like being interrogated. I wish I could note a tip: *Fast-talking is your job.* "So how much will it cost?" I repeat to keep this conversation professional and out of my business.

Ben stares at me for a moment. "I have a grandson your age." He nudges his head to the side. "I'll take you to Old Town. As for payment, I'll work with what you got."

"You will?" My voice cracks. My jaded senses give up. The risk is worse if I stay in this dingy town much longer. Wanda is watching me from the steps of her bus. After a pause, I wave off Wanda and briefly turn on my recorder with my back to the taxi driver.

"Tip: Believe your instincts. Trust your senses." I turn around and take Ben's offer with a handshake. "My name is Icabum."

CHAPTER 22

BEN

Once I settle onto the backseat of Ben's yellow taxicab #16, the tired, old gentleman proves to be quite the talker. I'm surprised I'm not bored. His voice has the steady tone of a guy you don't mind doing all the talking—just like my grandpa. I remove Enzo's jacket and tune in.

"I've been a taxi driver for over fifty years," he says as we pull onto the interstate. "You see a different world."

"How so?" I ask.

"People share a lot about themselves when they think they'll never see you again. It's amazing how many people need someone to listen and not judge them. I may drive a taxi, but I'm a part-time therapist."

"When you're not driving a taxi, what do you do?"

Ben shakes his head. "That's not how this works." His golden eyes catch mine in the rearview mirror. "I don't talk about myself." The dice ornament hanging from his mirror clinks together. *Heaven's Gate*, they say.

I pull out the saran-wrapped PB&J sandwich Mom made for my trip and offer up a triangle to Ben. His furry brows lift. He takes the piece through the window in the Plexiglas between us.

"Did your mom make this for you?" he asks before he takes a bite and gives a pleased smirk.

Tip, I jot down in my field notebook. *Don't forget to eat. Nothing too heavy, else a tempered stomach might spoil your case.*

I nod to Ben's question. Thinking of Mom tugs my lips into a frown. It won't be long before she finds out I'm missing. But she'll only worry for a few hours before I call from the train station and tell her I'm all right. My foot bounces. Ben watches me in the mirror.

"Does she know where you are?" he asks.

"Uh-huh," I mumble around my bite and then scratch excess peanut butter from my gums with my tongue.

I step on my foot to control my fidget. Ben stays quiet. The dice clink in the silence. The weight on my chest crawls up my throat until it sputters out of my mouth like a flat soda.

"I'm supposed to be on a bus to see my dad," I say. Ben nods. I suck on my lips for a moment and then shift forward. The cracked pleather seat beneath me crunches. "That's where my mom thinks I'm headed."

There's a long pause. "Since you're in my taxi," Ben says, "I'm assuming you've changed your plans."

"There's a Maltese Falcon I need to retrieve in Old Town."

His brows lift. "Maltese Falcon, huh? Like the Humphrey Bogart movie?"

I press against the Plexiglas dividing us. "You know about Bogart?"

"Bogart, Bacall, Stewart, Cagney, Robinson. Too many great actors and actresses to count during the Golden Age of Hollywood."

My face hurts from my grin. "I can quote every Bogart line in all seventy-five of his movies. But nothing is better than his role as Sam Spade."

"Any movie, you say?" Ben thinks for a moment. "Where were you last night?" he asks without taking his eyes off the road.

I bounce on my seat at the movie line he challenges me with, and then I freeze with a lazy look. "That was so long ago. I don't remember."

Ben's shoulders lift with a soft chuckle. "Will I see you tonight?"

I slap on my cocked-brow clenched-jaw Bogart expression. "I never make plans that far ahead."

A laugh bursts out of the taxi driver's mouth, completely changing the look of his tired face.

"Come on, Ben. *Casablanca*, 1942? Give me a challenge." *Casablanca* is my mom's favorite Bogart movie. She likes the mushy romance stuff, and we watch it every Tuesday night she has off.

"1942, huh?" Ben says. "I thought it was the year I was born."

"When was that?"

He gives a wry grin. I'm asking personal questions again. Instead, he says, "I was born the day before the attack on Pearl Harbor." Ben thinks this will roll right over my head. He doesn't know who he's dealing with.

"The attack was the morning of December 7, 1941," I say with little thought. "So, you were born on the 6th." Ben shows an impressed frown.

Watching vintage movies has sharpened my knowledge of history, especially when it comes to the first half of the twentieth century.

"Nope," I add. "Casablanca debuted November 26, 1942. But 1941 was a good year for classic films: Orson Welles's *Citizen Kane*, Cary Grant's *Suspicion*, and my favorite movie of all time, Humphrey Bogart's *The Maltese Falcon*."

"Does the movie have anything to do with the Maltese Falcon you need to retrieve?"

"Sort of," I answer vaguely, suspicious to let anyone know I'll be coming into a bunch of cash.

"So, where is this Maltese Falcon that I need to drop you off at?"

"A Classic Film Festival."

Ben nods. "Ah. It's making sense. Do you need to use my cell phone to tell someone you're almost there?"

I consider it for a moment. I have to save my walkie battery, and I don't need my friends calling the coppers when they don't hear from me after Bear Bottom. "Are you sure it would be okay?"

"Yeah. Make it quick, though."

"I'll just send a text if that's all right?" Enzo has his own cell phone already.

"Sure." Ben passes his phone. I thank him gratefully.

I stare at Ben's ancient Nokia phone. He has to walk me through how to text with it. I type in Enzo's number and get to work trying to text. My thumb cramps as I feverishly push on numbers to get to the letters I need. I finally send the message: *This Icabum. In taxi to Old Town. Tell others.* I hiss at the bad grammar, but my thumb couldn't take much more. I pass Ben back his cell phone and suggest an upgrade.

"Isn't *The Maltese Falcon* film inappropriate for a twelve-year-old?" Ben asks as he tosses his cell phone into his cup holder.

"Not at all. A tea party to today's standards. Sure, there are deaths, but there's never any blood. All suggestions and innuendos."

Ben nods.

I lean forward. "The lifestyle doesn't influence me if that's what you think." Ben is surely considering the constant smoking seen in the movie, but people just didn't know then. "Thank goodness for the Internet to make us all less ignorant." Tyler's favorite saying.

I continue, "Bubble-Yo gum gives the same look as cigarettes with the advantage of extending my shelf life instead of lowering it. I even got my grandpa to switch. I chew for Sam Spade. It's the one thing I wish he would have done differently. He'd have made chewing gum look good." The ultimate Gum Chew, for sure.

"If only he had you around," Ben says.

"If only." I grin. "But soda is my vice. I'm having trouble quitting." *Tip,* I write down. *Choose a comfort fidget, like swirling a can of soda. It's an excellent way to redirect your emotions so they don't show on your face.*

Ben tilts his head to show he's listening while keeping his eyes on the road. I'm compelled to keep talking. "I like the art of classic detective films: the lighting, the clothes, and the suspense. Sam Spade is my idol above idols.

I love him because—" Words get stuck in my throat, and it surprises me. I flop back against my seat.

Ben watches me in the mirror. I can see in his eyes that I have failed a standard tip. I sigh and write down *Tip: Fix your face. A detective has one look: bored.*

"Why is Sam Spade your favorite?" Ben asks.

I chew on the inside of my mouth. "He . . . he just told it how it is. You know, *life*. I wish I had someone who did that for me." My words are barely a whisper. Ben is quiet again. I clear my throat and flip this conversation to a subject I enjoy discussing. "And most importantly, he had incredible style."

"That makes two of you," Ben says. I smirk. "You sure know more than I did at your age. But then again, it was a different time."

"I pick up random facts like pennies. You never know when you'll need one." I pause and write that down as a tip too. "So," I say slowly, considering his comment about living in a different time. "What records did you listen to in the 1950s? Chuck Berry? Elvis Presley?" Ben stays quiet. I push on despite his *no talking about myself* rule. "Did you serve in Vietnam in the 1960s? Did you vote for John F. Kennedy or Richard Nixon?" Silence. "Did you use one of the first computers in the 1970s? What was it like? I bet it was terrible."

Ben waves his finger. No more questions about himself. I have a human time capsule in front of me, and he won't even answer one question. I lean back, but before I do, I spot a sleeping bag tightly rolled on the passenger side floor. I want to ask about it, but I know he won't answer that either.

We drive on in comfortable silence for an hour. The time allows me to tackle some tips for my essay. I skim through my notes that I've organized and filed. Doing so reminds me to add tips: *Neat note-taking*, and *Flawless filing*. I still have a long way to go if I want to hit one hundred.

"Doing homework?" Ben asks.

"Yeah," I reply, taking a break to pop M&Ms from my snack bag into my mouth. I rattle the bag to see if Ben wants any. He shakes his head. "I'm writing a guide on how to be a detective," I continue around a mouth full of candy. "A personal account."

"You're a detective?"

"I am. More like a private eye that sits outside the law. Mostly because I work better on my own."

"Like Sam Spade?"

"*Exactly*," I say with a little too much vigor. "I'm also not old enough to be part of Sheriff's police force. I do a lot of the dirty sniffing and call them in for backup." I remember the case of Mrs. Pomelo's suspiciously stinky couch. Under further investigation, I discovered the stolen cheese from the farmer's market.

"I see," Ben says as the taxicab's blinker clicks.

"My essay will have one hundred tips of the trade."

I get a thought and write down the word *Tip*. Before I finish, Ben says, "Do you take any suggestions?"

"Sure. What do you have?"

"Trust is like your heart. Don't give it willingly."

I stare at the back of his head for a moment, remembering my *Dad* case file. I push the thought away and write the tip slowly.

Looking back up, my eyes catch on a small slip of paper attached to the divider wall. It's Ben's taxi license—and it expired twenty-five years ago. My joints stiffen when I remember Ben's thumb was covering the expiration date on his license when he showed it at the depot. I look at the sleeping bag.

"Ben?" My voice warbles.

"Yeah?"

I swallow. "You're not really a taxi driver. Are you?"

CHAPTER 23

FAIR FARE

I brace myself for Ben to speed up. My mind swirls with thoughts on how best to eject myself from this moving vehicle. But the old man does nothing.

"I'm not going to hurt you, kid," he says.

"But—"

"Trust me."

"I trust no one. Not even my feet to do the walking."

"Good." He continues to drive steadily. "Do you know where I need to go once we get to Old Town?"

"Right here is fine." We're in the center lane of the freeway.

Ben looks in the mirror, his golden eyes squinting with humor. "You're a detective, right?"

"Yes." I lift my juddering chin.

"What would you have said to another kid lost in Bear Bottom?"

I lower my eyes and whisper, "Call the police."

"You focus too much on the road ahead of you and not the driver at the wheel."

"But you—"

"Not me . . . *you*. The one making all the decisions."

I squirm in my seat.

"My road changes daily," he continues, "but I know the driver." As I try to figure out what he means, he adds, "Now. Where to?" His finger is directed at the sign for Old Town gliding by.

I swallow a breath of excitement. My eyes drag slowly away from Ben to the crumpled ticket I've pulled from my pocket.

"It's at the Galagala Convention Center," I say. "But I don't want to trouble you anymore. Really, once we hit the town, drop me off. I'll find the way. What's this ride costing me anyway?" He said he would work with what I have.

"You have a choice," Ben replies. "The fare is at $94.86 right now."

I nearly swallow my gum. I don't have the money, but I cool my surprise. "You said I have a choice?"

Ben nods. "Yep. Pay the fare or give me your mom's phone number."

My neck starts to prickle with sweat. I check my expression and smooth out my voice when replying. "That's who I texted earlier."

Ben gives me a hard look in the mirror. "I haven't lied to you once. Don't lie to me."

I snarl at my lap. "Why do you want her number?" I mumble.

"Your mom deserves to know where you are."

"I'll pay the fee." I'll sell my clothes if I have to.

"Fee just increased to $150 for liars."

"What? I didn't . . . this is robbery!"

Ben flicks the automatic door locks up and then down. A threat.

The air in the taxicab thickens with my growing panic. "You need the money," I say.

"I don't need anything. Only to keep you safe." The words are cool against my face. It sounds like he means it.

My heel bounces. "Fine," I reply in the tone of a scolded child. Ben says nothing more. He's given me the price, and I have to pay it.

I check my pocket watch. Despite everything, I bob on my seat. 12:40 p.m. I'm here and twenty minutes early! I dig in my garment bag. The bow-tie I'm wearing is replaced with a long black tie. My Oxfords get an extra polish with a sheen like swimming seals. My EZ GEL'ed hair is tested for stiffness before replacing my fedora with an honorable tilt. A trench coat is shrugged on, more necessity than style.

Tip, I write. *Get a coat. One with deep pockets for your notebook, cash, granola bar, and bubblegum.* I fill my pockets with just that and more. I take Enzo's jacket, roll it in a tight ball, and place it on the floor at my feet. Enzo doesn't need it, but Ben might.

When I realize where I am, glee shoves me against the taxicab's window. Ben drove me straight to the Galagala Convention Center when I was distracted getting ready. The sight is so amazing that I squeal like someone gave me a free fedora hat.

"Holy Bogart!" I shout against the glass as Ben slows to a stop. And Bogarts there are. Dozens of them are in various stages of film legacy. A few Rick Blaines from *Casablanca* in white jackets and black bowties. A sprinkling of Philip Marlowes from *The Big Sleep* in trench coats like me. One Lieutenant Commander Philip Francis Queeg from *The Caine Mutiny* in a military uniform. There is even a bare-chested man with leeches all over him to look like Charlie Allnut from *The African Queen*. It is no surprise that there are a ton of Sam Spades. Men and women dressed as Bogart wait in a line that spans half a block to enter a door that reads *10th Annual Humphrey Bogart Costume Contest.* I glance at my pocket watch. The costume contest line looks long, so I decide to skip it for now. I need to figure out how to get in first.

"Right here is fine, Ben," I say, gasping for air. I tap on the door like a puppy wanting to be let out. He unlocks the door. I jerk it open.

Ben leans out of the window. "Fare, kid."

I blink out of awe and frown at Ben. I pull out my field notebook and jot down the number to my middle school. It's closed for spring break. No one will be there to catch his call. I feel a little guilty stiffing him after all he's done for me, but I don't need a call to Mom right now. Mom will know I'm missing in an hour when my dad goes to pick me up. Once I secure the prize, I'll call her from the train station. Gotta stick to the plan. I take out my leather wallet next.

"No money," he says.

"At least for gas, Ben—"

"Save it. You'll need it."

I pull out a business card to Farney Fig's Fit and Flare Tailor Shop instead and write on the back of it: *Good for one waistcoat. Charge to Icabum's credit.*

"Here, take this," I say. "It's where I work on the weekends. Next time you pass through Circle's End, come by for a waistcoat." Ben chuckles. Tip: Homely untidiness. As a human, you are obligated to refer someone to a good tailor.

"Oh!" I add and dig in my satchel to pull out the other half of my sandwich. It's smashed and wrapped haphazardly in saran plastic. "Take this."

Ben nods his thanks. "The phone number too," he says when he doesn't fall for the distraction of the other items. I rip my school's number from my notebook. Ben grabs his fare and stares at me for a second. His eyes are more intense than before, catching the honey haze of sunshine around him. "Those tips you are working on . . . don't let them sidetrack you while you're on your own. Your number one tip should be to know yourself before you can begin to understand others."

I drag my eyes to the ground and nod.

"I'm no Sam Spade, but I'm just telling you how it is." Ben pats my shoulder. "Here's looking at you, kid."

I smirk at the *Casablanca* movie quote. "I know nothing about you, but it's good to know there are people in this world like you."

Ben almost looks sad. "I'm not all that great either, kid, but I'm making up for it. I hope you find what you're looking for. Stay safe."

I nod, tighten my grip on my garment bag, and leave Ben and his taxicab to wade through a sea of Bogarts. I've done it. I'm really here. After everything that has gone wrong, lady luck might be sticking to my heel.

CHAPTER 24

DUCK SOUP

I open my walkie and whistle. "The bird is in the nest. Over."

There's static. "What bird? Over," answers Tyrone, loud music blares in the background. I forgot the Chokeberrys are at their auntie's birthday party.

"*Me*," I say. "I'm here. Over."

I smile when I hear the Chokeberrys gabble and cheer.

"I don't have a lot of power, so let's make this quick. I need to find a way in. Over."

"You should charge it—"

"Don't start. What's the lay of the land? The featured case is in Mystery Hall at the West Gate. Where's that? Over."

"It's west," likely said by Tyrone.

"Just give me directions to the featured case," I grumble. "And say *over*, so I know you're done speaking. Over." I scratch at my phantom beard. The crowd to the door is thickening. I push to stay on my feet and scan for my opportunity to sneak in.

"It's Tyler," I hear. "Inside the hall, go left. It starts in twenty minutes."

"Ooo-ver," inserts Tyrone.

I'm swallowed up by the mood of the festival. "Duck soup," I say with my thick detective talk. "I'm hitting on all eights. I'll be in and out of this joint with a clean sneak. Over."

"Huh?" Tyrone replies.

"You were supposed to memorize the list of terms I passed out at the last meeting. Over."

"Oh, right. Yeah, we lost those, so you'll have to speak English."

I growl. "Close your head and go climb a thumb," I say and hear Tyrone's loud hoot. "Enzo? Buddy, how are you doing?"

My stomach flips when he doesn't respond right away. "Okayf... Whaf's uf? Ofer," I finally hear.

I'm not surprised Enzo is eating. It's past noon. He's probably on his fourth meal. The kid can pack down food. "Are you safe back at home?"

There is a pause as he swallows. "Artie stopped at a street fair on our way to Jacksonville," drones Enzo's monotone voice.

"Jacksonville?" I shout and startle a few people around me.

"You're not saying over. Over," Tyrone probes with a snicker.

"Clam it you. Enzo?"

"We're down the street from your grandparents," mumbles my friend.

"Really?" My chest flares with pride. "I don't believe it. How—?"

"¿Estás bien, Icaboom?" a high female voice enters the speaker.

"Is . . . is that Paoula? Over." Enzo's nanny is like a second mother to him.

"Yeah," Enzo replies. "After I left you, I asked my parents if she and Artie could take me on a trip to Florida. They're staying near your grandparents all week. Cool if I stay with you? Uh . . . over."

I let out a tight breath with a chuckle. My face beams. Enzo's been to my grandparents' house in Florida with my mom and me a few times. He knows the address because of the chant we made one car ride.

"Heading to 35 Waterloo, where the sun is high and the cows moo. Over and around the hill, in the town of Jacksonville.

To eat grandma's tasty treats and smell grandpa's stinky feet.

To fish in the bay and sing 'Come sail away.'

How much longer could it be? Oh, boy, do I have to pee!"

"Absolutely!" I say. "I'll let you know when I'm on my way. I know my grandpa will be happy to see us." Sick or not, seeing us will bring more cheer than a phone call. Grandpa Gilbert thinks Enzo is some sort of fish whisperer. Fish fight to get on his hook. I can't believe this. Enzo and I will spend spring break together with my grandpa. I better not screw up today.

"¿Llamaste a tu madre?"

"What'd she say, Enzo?" I ask.

"Watch out for llamas on the mattress." I ignore Tyrone. He adds, "Signing off. Our dad's coming. Good luck."

"Paoula asked if you called your mom," Enzo replies.

"*Enzo*, you told them?" I try to whisper.

"No. Your mom called at 11:30 looking for you. I told her I thought you were on a bus. Nothing else. She called my parents, who told her I was with Artie and Paoula."

"She called?" I've stopped walking. Okay, don't worry. He said I was on a bus, which could still mean I'm on bus #32. Why did she call? 11:30 was when I transferred buses at Thomasberg. Mom isn't supposed to know I'm missing yet. Maybe it's lingering suspicion from the car ride, and she's checking her snares.

"Enzo," I say. "If she calls again, let me know. I better get into this place. And Tyler's dumb battery is on its last bar. Over and out." I slam the case shut.

Why would Mom call Enzo? What's tipped her off? My mom's shadow follows me like a dark rain cloud waiting to wash away everything. I mute the thought for now to begin the greatest case of my life, but first I have to get in.

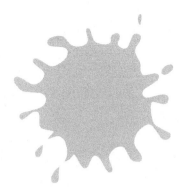

CHAPTER 25

HEAVEN'S GATE

Some people imagine heaven with cherubs and puffy clouds. Heaven found its way to Earth at the Galagala Convention Center, stock full of legends in smart suits. I throw myself into character and saunter through a slow rolling fog of wreathing gloom, supplied from a machine nearby.

"Tip: Sport a proper cock-eyed grimace. It's a trained skill." I display just that. If not done properly, you might get redirected to the nearest restroom.

There is no head without a hat as it used to be and should be. From double-breasted suits and trench coats to fluffy furs and strong-shouldered silhouettes, women and men didn't just show up, they brought the show. At the threshold of the convention center, surrounded by golden glitz, gangsters, and gumshoes, I listen to trumpets swooning as I wait to travel back in time to an cra frozen in movie history.

In the long line, I search for an opportunity to get in. I'm behind two men dressed like a disheveled, down-on-his-luck screenwriter and a leaching playboy. Behind me is a black-dressed vixen who keeps calling me *sweetheart*.

Bingo, I think, smirking at the woman.

The bulky security guards at the door, holding black instrument cases to resemble classic gangsters, eye me as I approach the front door. One man whispers to the other, who then leaves. I push away gloom and doom and become the part.

"Tip: Quick talk and spin an easy smile," I whisper into the recorder as I turn back to the woman behind me.

I clear my throat to get the woman's attention and to gravel up the whistle of puberty in my voice. With my best Sam Spade impression, I say, "You look like a lady who knows where she's going."

Without skipping a beat, she says, "Sweetheart, there ain't a place I haven't been." Oh, she's good.

"Care to go nowhere with me then? A short man like me doesn't have far to fall."

The woman breaks out of character to laugh. She reaches out a black-gloved arm to me. "Name's Kitty."

"Like the cat. I like that. Name's Sam Spade." I pat her out-stretched knuckle.

She grins. I wet my whistle and display my easy smile. Another skill that takes practice not to look ill.

"Come on," I say, still in character. "It takes two to get in trouble." I make a mental note to add that as a tip. This place is going to be magic for my essay.

I loop my arm in hers and wince because I've got it backward. Kitty looks like she is leading me, a mother dragging her son. Too late to change. We're at the door now.

"You two together?" security asks.

"Don't give her any ideas," I reply with a lazy sneer, but it waffles under the man's heated stare.

"Step aside a second, kid," the man says. *Nine horns of hades,* I curse to myself.

I look at Kitty with pleading eyes. She sucks on her bright red lips in thought and then heaves a breath.

"Are you going to keep my brother long?" she says. "I'm leaving him with you if this means I miss the singsong sing-a-long."

The big man looks down at me, and I pretend to look irritated with Kitty when I want to hug her. I drag my eyes to him. "Fine. I'll stay here. Do you like magic? I'm really good at magic." Tip: Choose a skill for distraction. "I have this one trick where I can stretch a bottle. Do you have an empty bottle and five bucks? The bottle is for the trick. The five bucks are for me." I fake a laugh.

The man purses his lips. "Go on," he says with a head nudge. "You look like someone. Had to stop you."

"I get that more often than you'd think," I chirp as I hurry to Kitty's side. Once through, my legs wobble with relief.

Kitty says, "You be good, little man."

"Play nice, Kitty," I reply and rush off when I spot the coat check.

"Checking your coat, kiddo," says the twenty-something dame working the counter.

"Nah, I'm keeping the coat," I answer. "I'd like to check my luggage, please."

"Who are you here with?"

"Trouble and a bag of names." I grin.

She snorts a laugh. "What's your name?"

"Sam Spade."

"Already have a Sam Spade here today. Got another name?"

"But I'm Sam Spade!"

"Sorry, kid. We can only have one person per name to check any items."

I frown and consider another alias. "Valentine." Bogart played a man named Valentine in three different movies.

"Got all three Valentines too."

"Philip Marlowe?" The name of Humphrey Bogart's other great detective character in *The Big Sleep*.

"You're in luck. Welcome, Marlowe." The girl takes my satchel and garment bag and returns with a ticket. The weight loss is a relief.

"If you take good care of those," I say, "I have a George and a Lincoln for you." A quarter and a penny, not a dollar and a five, but she doesn't need to know that yet.

"How about I lock them up?" she says.

"Appreciated." I place the ticket and my wallet in the inside pocket of my trench coat for safekeeping, where my handful of Bubble-Yo gum, recorder, and walkie are.

I unwrap a fresh nub of Bubble-Yo and toss it in my mouth. I share some gum with folks nearby. "Tip," I say to them. "Cigarettes aren't a fashion worth reviving, like sunbathing without sunscreen and hitchhiking. Bubble-Yo is the way to go."

I gnaw on my gum, making my character grimace fiercer, as I head across the convention lobby in pursuit of my great case. This cat's only got so many lives left.

CHAPTER 26

THE CASE

Inside Mystery Hall, I freeze at the top of the steps leading down to the main room and swallow an awe-filled sob. Vendors fill the floor with vintage memorabilia, one-of-a-kind gifts, and free swag. The air oozes with perfume and innuendos, pushed around by a melodic croon from a young Frank Sinatra impersonator and a piano player.

Unrestrained eagerness throws me out of character. I scamper down the steps and poke my nose between people to see into every booth. Custom candles with unique scents of Disenchanted Daisies and Wasteland's Winter Wallows. Perfumes with names like "Imperiled Iris" and "Embittered Euphorbia." Vintage mystery novels with classic detective characters from John Dickerson Carr's Gideon Fell to Agatha Christie's Hercule Poirot and Miss Marple.

Barbers expertly cut hair into classic styles known as the Contour and Boogie and wrap warm towels around freshly shaven faces. I rub my fingers along my cut chin and watch them work. A man acting as a journalist snaps my picture with a vintage camera. I wince when the flashbulb explodes with smoke and light. Other people record him with their cell phones.

By the end of the first row, I have a sack full of freebies. I need to find the featured case at the West Gate, but I feel like I'm in a fairy-induced hypnotic trance, unable to break free as the years fly by outside this hall.

A large Sam Spade image towers over me. I squeak. The movie poster reads *The Maltese Falcon* playing in the East Theater at 2:30 p.m. I have to see that. When will I ever get to see my favorite movie of all time on the big screen? And it will be done in time to get to the train station by five o'clock. I check my pocket watch. That gives me an hour and a half to solve the case.

I rush down the second aisle, looking for a way to the West Gate. A food stand named Donut Trust Me gets my attention. I should fuel up before the case. The baker's special is a massive white-powdered donut with red jam filling that he calls The Bloody Anti-Hero. I get one and chomp bites while looking for a way out of this bliss.

A man shouts through the PA system like an old-time police radio. I blink out of my daze and listen with the donut to my lips. "Calling all private eyes. The Great Whatsit is missing. Five minutes until the case begins. The first to solve the mystery will receive the coveted Maltese Falcon trophy and $1,000. Five rooms of clues, two scenes, one interview. Free to enter. Space is limited. Line up starts outside the West Gate. We need the best of the best. We need you, Icabum."

He didn't really say my name, but I added it in my mind. I trash the rest of my donut and rip the big napkin from out of my collar as I sprint to the West Gate, weaving in and out of fishnet stockings, pleated trousers, and the occasional jingle-brain in jeans. I remind myself that I have an hour and a half until the movie starts. That's plenty of time to solve this case. I've solved others during a lunch break at school.

"File into the staging room," a man shouts with a tired, grumbled drawl. He's sitting at a wooden desk that says *Lieutenant Rockford Cracow* on a shiny, golden placard. Cracow clasps his hands on his desk to hold up his weary slouch. He's wearing a white dress shirt with rolled sleeves, a loose wool tie, and black suspenders. A cane is resting beside his desk. The guy is in his early thirties but holds the character of a seasoned man of the law. "You'll hear a phone call over the speaker," he continues to the crowd watching his show. "Then you have free reign of four rooms to look for clues until it is your turn to interrogate the suspect in the fifth room. You'll get a number on your way in. When it's called, head into the interrogation room."

I pat myself to make sure my walkie, field notebook, and recorder are easy to get to. Cracow eyes me curiously. Lieutenants and private eyes play on two sides of the same coin, but this could be because I look like I don't have a chaperone. I slip forward between two men in sharp suits and laugh loudly at something trivial one says. It gets me past Cracow.

"Mayday! Mayday!" says the muffled voice of a Chokeberry through my walkie. I jolt with surprise and cough as I press a hand to quiet its sound.

I take my number and look over my shoulder once more as I move to the staging room. Cracow stares at me and mumbles something I can't hear into his walkie.

"Mayday! Mayday!" returns the voice in my walkie.

I yank it from my pocket, flip it open, and push the button. "Contest starting. Can't talk. Over," I murmur under my breath so the people walking nearby can't hear.

"Ick!" yells Tyler. Static crackles loudly, followed by a sharp kickback that makes me wince. I can't figure out how to turn it down, so I step away from the crowd. "Ick," he repeats. "Your mom—ju—by—er." Static hisses. He repeats it, but it breaks up worse. I smack the metal container.

"Tyler, I can't hear you. Over."

"Your mom came by! She knows—you're missing, Ick. She's—" There's no more fizzle, pop, or hiss. Not another word. The walkie is dead. Regardless, I hiss Tyler's name into the walkie like a fool. A woman stops to ask if I'm okay because all she sees is a kid yelling at his Altoids.

I nod at her curtly and glance over my shoulder. Cracow is back on his walkie. I scurry into the staging room, cursing PG-13 words to myself.

My mom knows I'm missing. It's early. Too early. I had thirty more minutes. I prepared for her to look for me, but it still fills me with dread.

I slap my cheek. Focus. I need to win this contest as fast as I can. That darkening cloud named Freyda Plum is out there, thundering through the skies.

I will win this. I have to.

I drag in a deep breath and then again a second time because the first one was tight and wheezed. I slap my face once more and look at the number written on my paper: *21*. I have to wait for twenty people until I can interrogate . . . who exactly?

CHAPTER 27

GREAT WHATSIT

I cram myself into the contest staging room near the farthest door to be the first person out. I stash my swag bag in the corner, hoping no one takes it before I'm done, and then wait for the call to play out. Most people don't even notice me as they chatter excitedly over my head.

The lights dim. A spotlight shines down on us. We hear a phone ring. It clicks as if someone answers. The speaker crackles with the clarity of an old receiver when a man speaks. I rush to turn on my recorder and leave it hidden in my pocket.

"Where have you been?" the gruff voice says. It sounds familiar. "I've been looking all over for you. Libertine Justice is at the police station. She won't let me near her and will only talk to you about the location of the Great Whatsit. Check the apartment for evidence and stop by the casino to talk to Chief before heading in. It might help. If you find the box, whatever you do, don't open it. Bring it straight to me." The voice's owner finally clicks. It's Cracow.

The Great Whatsit. The mystery box from *Kiss Me Deadly*! I know this movie. Is it as easy as looking for the box? Cracow said not to open it. Will I be able to resist not looking into it after all these years of desperately wanting to know what was inside? Is this box what's standing between me and the Maltese Falcon trophy?

I scribble down keywords from the call in my field notebook as the door opens behind me and the contest begins. People shove past with animated conversations. When I finish writing the details of the call, I push between hips and scan the dimly lit hallway.

The details used to make it look like an old movie freezes me with wonder: glass chandeliers, Persian rugs, and oil paintings. All the saturated colors are muted by shadows. People wander around and take pictures, but I don't have time to dillydally. I need to solve this case quickly so I can smooth over Mom's fury with a thousand bucks in my hand.

Cracow put himself behind a new desk at the end of the hall to the right. Deskmen like him are ten a penny. I didn't like the way he looked at me. I keep my distance by heading left.

Win. I have to win. The words repeat like a melodic chant.

I murmur some tips into my recorder as I charge past three doors to get to the farthest one, flooding with inspiration from the hunt to solve the case.

"Tip: Don't forget federal, local, and natural laws apply to you. You're a stone, but not indestructible. Tip: Honesty and ethics. Use them when the opportunity allows you to be honest and ethical." A couple asks me to take a picture of them in front of a fireplace. I don't answer and keep walking.

"Tip . . . fighting is overrated. No need to fight if you are two steps ahead. Tip: Master the slap. If you are forced to fight, one solid slap with a flat palm to a suspect's cheek will leave them stunned long enough to get you out of there."

I have to pause a minute behind a few people who shuffle into the first room. Enough time to review my notes on this case.

Libertine at station. She won't let Cracow near her. Will only talk to me about the location of the Great Whatsit. If the box is found, don't open it. Bring the box to Cracow.

I wipe a sweaty brow. "Tip: Answers are in the details."

The neatly worded phone call didn't give me much. Five rooms, two scenes, and one interrogation—they might help to decode a hidden message in the call. Everyone here is in my way to $1,000. I need to win this. For Mom . . . and Grandpa Gilbert too. Our mutual love of classic movies will help me today. I turn up my senses, wash my face with vigilance, and spit out a swig of doubt. Let the games begin.

CHAPTER 28

APARTMENT

The door at the end of the hallway opens into a decorated 1940s studio apartment with fresh light blue walls. It's designed straight out of the golden age of classic film, super lavish right down to the floral living room set in colors of eggplant, gray, and yellow. A dressing table of satin, ruffles, and roses matches the iron post bed beside it. The whole place is sweet and tough at the same time, like a bag of hard candy.

This is the apartment Cracow mentioned. Who does it belong to? I think as I sniff it out. The lighting is low. Fake moonlight outside the window casts a grid shadow along the linoleum floor. An old dial radio is crackling in the corner with updates on the troops overseas.

"After a month-long battle with Japanese forces," the reporter says sharply. "Allied troops have captured the island of Iwo Jima in the western Pacific."

I tap into my well of historical knowledge. World War II is my specialty, a common theme in my favorite movies. "Tip," I say to my breast pocket, where my recorder is still running. I plan to keep it on. "Know the difference between punditry and pungency. Big words, but one makes you wiser while the other stinks."

The radio repeats the announcement. It's on a loop, so it must be important. I think hard, bullying my bubblegum as I do.

Iwo Jima. Grandpa Gilbert's favorite actor, John Wayne, played Sergeant John Stryker in the Sands of Iwo Jima. "Into each life, a little rain must fall," Stryker said. Not important. Focus, Icabum. 1949 was the year of the movie, not the year of the capture. Year of the capture . . . 19 . . . 45! We are in 1945. After March in the year 1945. I wring my hands and look around. Did anyone else figure that out yet?

World War II not only changed the lives of soldiers but also the lives of people at home. Style, lifestyle, and other stuff. While the men were overseas, more women headed out to the workforce. I search the room for those sorts of changes to see who I'm dealing with.

A woman lives here . . . a working woman. Jewels like ice are on the dressing table. A woman with money who likes to buy nice things. Assumed to be Libertine's apartment but not confirmed. No appliances. Eats out. I squint at the fake moonlight streaming through the window. It's night, and the woman's not here. Out with someone? The news loop might mean she's keeping tabs on a man on the frontline, or it's just to let the contestants know the year. A small clock confirms the time. Eleven o'clock. I'm standing in 1945 at 11:00 p.m.

A dozen handsomely-dressed men and women stroll through the room, compromising the scene. "Tip," I whisper to my recorder. "Organize the scene, even if it's not your scene to organize. Tip: Reconstruct the events of the crime to see how the dominoes fell." I walk the studio, slow like a creeping cat, sorting tips and evidence. "Tip: Power of deduction is strengthened with logic and critical thinking."

I look behind a curtain, nudge my shoe against the leg of the couch, and glance under a lampshade. "Tip," I murmur and chomp on my gum. "Crime will require all your senses . . ." I pause and sniff the air. "The smell of honeysuckle like the movie *Double Indemnity*, 1944, the taste of poison like *D.O.A. Dead on Arrival*, 1949, or even the sound of screeching tires like in . . . every movie."

It *is* honeysuckle I smell. A perfume bottle confirms it. I drag a finger along a glossy pink table. The occupant is possibly female, lives alone, or her partner likes the same powder-puff pink. I freeze. There are too many people in this room to get a good read, but at my short height, I have a view the others don't. I turn and casually back up to the fake front door's mail slot, where I see the tip of an envelope visible through the grate. When no one's looking, I lift the metal flap, snatch the envelope, and shove it into my pocket. No one said anything about taking evidence. It might slow the others down. It's a foul move, but these kids don't have their mothers after them.

More people pour into the room. It's time for me to scram before curious eyes look my way. "Double tip: know how long to boil an egg and know when the goose is cooked."

CHAPTER 29

ALLEY

The hallway is too crowded to read the letter, so I hit the second room to see if there is a quiet spot. The PA system announces *number 6* for the interrogation room. I have a while to go until my questioning with Libertine Justice.

The doorway spits me into a fake back alley, complete with the sounds of taxi horns and rumbling trains passing overhead. The left wall is a landscape image of New York's skyline. The sidewalk drops into a real-looking gutter full of trash. The lights are low except for three streetlamps to my right that glow against a brick apartment building façade. A single metal fire escape zigzags to a window where a TV plays. The TV replays a scene inside of an apartment. Several contestants look up at the screen and watch the scene unfold. I join them.

"You never wanted it. Never!" a woman shouts. All that can be seen are the silhouettes of a man and a woman arguing, but the window frame cuts off their heads, so you can't make out their faces.

My shoulders slouch. Something about the yelling brings up one of the last memories of my parents before the *Dad* case five years ago. The thought of my dad waiting at the station cheers me up a little. Or did he even make it there before my mom called him? I frown at the thought of my mom frantically looking for me.

The man grips the woman's forearm and says, "I asked for it!"

"No, you didn't," she hisses. "You expected it."

"So, instead, you gave it to someone who collects them like trading cards."

I hold my recorder in the air to catch every word.

"If he finds out you came looking for it, he'll kill you," the woman says.

"I'd rather die," the man replies. "It hurts worse not to have it."

The video plays over again, and I listen once more.

"I'm sure that's cheating," a voice says behind me. I flinch and turn.

A girl in her early twenties with an easy smile grins at me. I take her in. She has on a fitted black jacket, pleated black trousers, a white button-down shirt, and a short black tie. Her dark curly hair is tucked in the fedora hat she has carelessly tilted on her head. A style to match the slouch she's holding.

"It's not cheating," I say, looking up at her and tucking my recorder back in my pocket. "I'm using my resources." I flash her a tight grin.

"Smart," she replies and nudges her head to the looping video. "What do you think it means?"

I eye her warily and chomp on my gum for a moment. This cat's my competition. She could be pumping me for information. I shrug and start to turn away. She's become a distraction. I have to keep moving.

"You know what I think?" she says.

Curiosity tugs my head back to her. "What?"

"I think we're assuming we have only one view." She glances up at the fire escape.

A smile pinches my cheek. "Tip: There's always more than one way to get an answer," I mumble to my recorder before turning fully toward her. "I normally work alone . . ."

"Me too," she replies coyly. "I guess we just happen to be heading in the same direction."

I chomp on my gum and wave a hand. "After you."

The woman nods and shoves her hands in her pockets as she saunters through the cluster of people watching the video. Once we climb the fire escape, she flops down on the top step. I sit next to her.

"Do you have a name?" I ask.

"It depends on who's asking," she replies.

"Cynicism is a good look on you."

The woman laughs out loud. "Big word for a kid."

"I make it a point to know things."

She nods. "Sam is my name. Sam Spade."

I jerk back. This must be the person from the coat check who stole my name. "Marlowe," I finally say. "Philip Marlowe." We shake hands, and our Bogart bond is sealed.

"How old are you?" she asks.

"I'm a vintage wine that ages well."

Sam laughs her nice laugh again. "Well, if I had to guess, I'm twelve years the wiser." She nudges my side.

The letter from the apartment is hot in my pocket as we look down at the alley. The sound of a railcar thunders through the speakers. It feels like they've heated this room for effect. It's working. A sticky layer of perspiration covers my face. I glance at Sam, who is scrutinizing the people below.

"Everyone's a suspect," she says, looking distracted.

I grin, think for a moment, and then whisper to myself, "Include that tip."

"Huh?"

I look away from her, feeling a little embarrassed. "I'm writing an essay with tips on how to be a detective. I'll include: Everyone's a suspect. It's a good one to remember at Thanksgiving dinner. I will give you credit."

She laughs and goes back to work, looking around the room for clues.

One of the most important tips of the trade comes to mind. I push it away, but it keeps coming back. I chew on my lip and allow myself to consider it. *Tip: Get a partner.* Enzo is always with me. I've never had another partner, and I can't imagine myself with another one. I trust no one else in this world more than my best friend. He'd want me to move on if it meant solving my great case. I'm hard-boiled, but something about Sam feels all right.

"Four eyes are better than two," I say casually, testing the water.

"Are you asking me to be your partner?"

My cheeks burn at her forwardness. I nod stiffly, shifting my eyes anywhere but at her. Sam's hand flashes in front of my face, positioned for an acceptance shake. I smirk and shake her hand.

"Split the $1,000 winnings?" I say tightly. $500 is still a lot and worth the sacrifice to save time with Mom hot on my heels. "The trophy is mine, though."

Sam considers me for a moment before she replies, "Sure."

I hurry and reach into my pocket to pull out the letter.

Sam's brows shoot up. "Where'd you get that?"

"In the apartment's mail slot."

"Well, let's check it out!" she says with hushed excitement.

I turn to her to block onlookers. I sniff it first. "Honeysuckle," I say. "Just like the apartment." The envelope is addressed to Libertine Justice, written in a flourished script.

"Dang," Sam says, stretching the syllable of the word. "The apartment is Libertine's."

I give her an impressed frown. I'd guessed as much as well, especially after seeing the place. I pause to pull out a fresh Bubble-Yo and pass one to Sam. "Detectives chew bubblegum where I come from," I add when I lift the wrapped gum to her.

Sam snatches it and spins the gum out of the wrapper. Together, we gnaw on our gum with tough-looking grimaces. "Go on. Open the envelope," she urges when I pause too long.

I feel like Charlie Bucket holding a candy bar just before he unwraps it and finds his Golden Ticket to Willy Wonka's Chocolate Factory. I knew I should have taken my evidence kit and rubber gloves out of my satchel. Too late to worry about it now. My finger slips along the flap, and it pops open. Slowly, I remove a neatly folded paper. I let out a breath. Sam leans in.

The note says *It's mine, Libertine Justice.*

Sam's brows crinkle. "If the envelope wasn't addressed to Libertine, the way the letter is written it looks like it was signed by her."

She's right. It's hard to tell, but I have to take it as a threat right now. I reread the elegant swooping script and put the letter back in my pocket. I scan the alley one last time. "This view is giving me nothing," I say. "And it's starting to get too crowded in here. Have you been to any of the other rooms?"

Sam wags her head.

"When is your interview?"

"My number is super high," she answers. "I have a while."

"I'm number 21," I say. "Let's get out of here. Besides the video, it's just the cityscape and the gutter." We pop up out of our seats and hurry down the metal stairs. Sam slips.

I snatch her hand. "Tip: Stick your neck out for nobody. But a hand? Yes."

Sam nods. "Let's take the gutter to avoid the crowd," she observes, leading the way. Our Oxfords crush newspapers and trash.

"Hold up, Sam," I shout over another train passing.

Sam turns with a smile but frowns when she sees what's in my hand. She tilts her head. "Why are you holding trash?"

"Do you think it's important that the date on this newspaper says April 12 when today is actually April 13?"

Sam is at my side in a blink. *The New York Times* newspaper headline screams *PRESIDENT ROOSEVELT IS DEAD. TRUMAN TO CONTINUE POLICIES*. Dated April 12, 1945. The radio in the apartment mentioned Iwo Jima, which happened in March of 1945. Connection? Possibly.

"This alley is yesterday," Sam says, looking up at the looping video. "This is a flashback."

I consider the video again. Flashbacks are common in classic films. "That must be Libertine up there in her apartment."

"The man might be the one who wrote the letter."

I shake my head. "I'm not thinking so. Something about the writing is too feminine."

"Or made to look that way." Sam wiggles her brows.

I check my pocket watch. 1:45 p.m. We've wasted too much time here.

"Got someplace else to be?" she adds.

"No. We have a contest to win. Tip: Determination. Keep your purpose firm like a well-pumped bike tire." I pause to listen to the number announced for the interrogation room. Number 13. "Let's go."

CHAPTER 30

GARAGE

C lusters of people exchange clues in the hallway. Sam and I push through to the third door. This is a smaller room than the others and has been made to look like a garage. The most notable thing in the place is the glossy black 1940s Pontiac Torpedo car that a dozen people are ogling over. Everyone here seems more interested in examining the car than the evidence. The two front doors of the vehicle are open, and so are the trunk and the hood. I'm too short to get a good look.

"Squeeze in," Sam says with a nudge on my shoulder.

I don't hesitate to push between people's hips to get to the driver's seat. A man in a pinstripe suit is testing out the wheel while another man sputters mechanic talk. I growl. The back window is down. In thoughtless action, I crawl through it, ignoring shouts from the spectators. I suppose I could have tried the back door, but I have no time.

I pop up in the backseat and search the car. Nothing. It's a show car. Pristine condition. No stains, no footprints. There are dozens of smudges and fingerprints, but they could be from any of these fools tampering with the evidence.

I'm about to crawl out when a man says, "Do you think it turns on?"

"We'd fill this place with exhaust if we did," replies the man in the driver's seat. "A shame though. I'd really like to hear it purr."

"They're talking like they have the—" My eyes snap to the ignition. "Keys!" Why would there be keys if we shouldn't turn it on?

"Excuse me." I lunge over the seat and yank the keys from the ignition, ignoring more shouts at me. I see Sam's fist pump within the crowd. Thirteen keys, including the car key, plus a dice keychain. Maybe they're keys to something in another room.

I shift out of reach of a rogue hand stretching through the window to grab the keys. I start to shove the keys in my pocket but freeze. The dice keychain is attached to the main ring. At first, I thought it was attached to the second key ring on the loop. No, that one has nothing on it. These keys aren't for something. They are thirteen unlucky keys left behind. Their purpose is to show something is missing from it. I toss the keys on the driver's lap and crawl out of the car, taking the proper way this time.

Sam is waiting for me. Her arms are crossed over her chest. Her lips are twisted with a smug look. "You're a Renaissance type, aren't you? Jack of all trades, master of none."

I snort and pull her away from the crowd toward a metal worktable on the opposite side of the room from the car. "More like a life hacker." I murmur into my recorder, "Note those as tips."

Sam chuckles. "What'd you find?"

"Something's missing from the key ring."

"Who does the car belong to? The trunk is empty. I checked." She examines the worktable that is filled with tools.

Someone handy, I think. I stop her reach. "Don't touch," I say, examining the table.

"Oh, right." Sam shoves her hands in her pockets to mimic me.

"Tip: Limit your blinking, so you don't miss anything." Also used in one of my *Anatomy of a Stakeout* podcast episodes.

"How do you keep track of all your tips?"

I tap my temple. "I have a memory like a fly trap. Things just stick."
Sam smiles.

I eye a crumpled calendar hanging on the wall next to a picture of
Rita Hayworth, a famous classic film actress. I wait for a pair of women
evaluating the table to pass and hurry to the calendar. *March 1945*, it reads.
Same as the radio. Another flashback.

"Whatever went missing has been gone since last month," I say,
pointing at the calendar.

"Do you think it's the Great Whatsit?"

"I think we're getting closer." *Closer* . . .

I lean into the calendar and poke at where it is dented in the center. I
swing the calendar to the side, revealing a hole smashed through the wall.

"Someone punched this calendar last month," I say, "and damaged
the drywall behind it."

"When the suspect noticed the Great Whatsit missing?"

I nod, deep in thought. "Tip: Scrupulousness. A big word about little
details," I mumble.

I've been chewing on my gum so hard my jaw is starting to hurt. The
producers of this contest have set up a lot of action off scene, a familiar style
of classic films. It's like a comic book when all you see is *KABLAM!* and
you know someone has been hit without actually seeing it happen. When
something is done off camera, people often refer to it as *in the gutter*.

I feverishly blink like I do when my mind is racing out of control. "In
the gutter," I sputter. Sam straightens her slouch. I look up into her eyes. "In
the gutter!" I snatch her hand and pull her after me back to the alley. "Tip:
One step back can be better than running two steps forward."

With little to see in the alley, most people have come and gone. Only
one couple is watching the loop when we head back in. I slide to a stop
inside the door and search the fake gutter with my eyes first.

Sam, in showing her skill as a master detective's partner, says to the
couple, "Have you checked out the car next door?"

"A clue?" the man asks excitedly.

"No, but the car is a beauty. Pontiac Torpedo."

The woman's eyes light up. The couple hurries out.

Sam flashes me a grin. "I'll watch the door. Hurry now!"

A long-lost smile fills my face. I rush along the fake gutter, sliding my feet and kicking trash out of the way. My feet *tap, tap, tap*, and then they *thunk*. I fall to my knees. My body rushes with adrenaline. The producers of this contest haven't slacked on details, so why put a sewage drain with a grate? I push trash out of the way and can barely control my hoot. I jerk on the metal grate and pull it up. Something in the hole catches my eye. I reach in and take it out.

In my hand sits a small Plexiglas box. Inside the box is an egg timer with twenty minutes left on the clock. The ticking is silenced by the railcars clambering and the video looping.

Sam mumbles a fancy curse word and apologizes. "You've found it. You've found the Great Whatsit."

I stare at the egg timer with a frown. I should be excited, but something doesn't feel right. "The call said don't open the box and bring it straight to Cracow." But there wasn't even a way to open it. It's glued shut.

In the movie *Kiss Me Deadly*, the Great Whatsit inside the box is never described. It is only thought to be threatening and becomes an obsession of people around it. Grandpa Gilbert explained that its existence was simply a fact, not something they could hold. What I hold now is dwindling time.

Sam reads my face. "What's wrong?"

"Too many things. Tip: Cause & correlation. One doesn't always mean the other." When sixth grader Honey Chestnut started getting A's on her Math tests, if she chewed Green Alien Atomic Chew bubblegum during her exams, she correlated her A's to the gum, but it wasn't the cause of her A's. It was, however, the cause of her mouth glowing green for two months.

I pop to my feet with a grunt and shove the palm-sized box into my deep trench coat pocket. "The Great Whatsit fits on a key ring," I say. "This box could have stayed here until it buzzed, and then what? No one would hear it. This is counting down to something, but the Great Whatsit is still out there." I listen to the video loop one more time.

"You never wanted it. Never!" the woman I suppose to be Libertine says.

"I asked for it!" replies the man I assume to be the angry Pontiac owner who's missing something.

"No, you didn't," she hisses. "You expected it." *It . . . it . . . it,* I think. *Possibly the missing something.*

"So, instead, you gave it to someone who collects them like trading cards." Libertine had the something and gave it away to someone who collects them. A collector.

"If he finds out you came looking for it, he'll kill you." *Another man . . . the collector Libertine gave something to.*

"I'd rather die. It hurts worse not to have it."

It's mine, Libertine Justice, the note from the apartment said. The hole in the wall was for losing it. The evidence is not clicking together. "Think, Icabum, think."

Sam gently touches my shoulder. I flinch out of thought. "One more room," she says.

"One more room," I repeat. When number 17 is announced for the interrogation room, we start to run.

CHAPTER 31

CASINO

I jerk to a stop when I exit the fake alley. The security guard who gave me trouble when I first entered this joint is at Cracow's desk. Lieutenant Cracow favors his right leg as he moves around to talk to the man privately.

"Sam, get in front of me," I say. My hat is lowered over my brows. My trench coat collar is pushed up high on my neck.

"What?" Sam says as she tries to see me, but I keep shuffling behind her. "Why? What's happening? Are you in trouble?"

"I always have one foot in trouble," I reply. Ain't it the truth? "We're too close to solving this. We need to win. Trust me and block."

Sam is too thin to cover me completely, but she pulls a fantastic move by sliding an arm across a woman's shoulder nearby. The two women cackle, and at the same time, make a perfect wall. At the fourth door, I slip in unnoticed by Cracow and the henchman. Sam saunters in proudly behind me. I pat her on the shoulder for her good work.

My mouth unhinges when I take in the new room. Sam throws another colorful curse word out and again apologizes for it. We've walked into a large casino, complete with roulette tables, a long, oiled bar, and a woman moaning melancholy blues without a band. She looks like she's eating the microphone, but that was how it was back then.

"Where do we even start?" Sam asks, seeming a little put out. The room is packed with people. Most look like contestants who have given up and are enjoying the bar too much.

"We're still missing the last scene. The phone call said to find Chief." The crowded room makes it hard to see. "There!" I throw my pointer finger at a spot across the room where a heavier-built man scratches his chin. People are near him, taking notes. Sam and I weave through the tables and the playful chatter.

"Quinlan," a male contestant says to the one I guessed was Chief. "What happened?"

My eyes gleam with the comparison of the man's looks as the movie legend Orson Welles to his character's name in *Touch of Evil*, 1958. I rattle my head. This contest has too many distractions. If I weren't in such a hurry, I'd want to live here.

I poke my head through the last line of people in front of Quinlan. I grab Sam's hand and pull her with me. "Tip: Interview in a group to watch other's reactions." She nods.

Quinlan speaks with throaty grunts. "It was like this when I arrived at the scene this morning. Happened sometime last night." In the corner where everyone is looking lies a busted cabinet with glass shattered all over the checkered floor.

"Is that the only thing broken?" I butt in with the question, annoying the other contestant. "Anything taken out of it?"

"Just the cabinet was broken. Nothing was taken." Not a robbery. The Great Whatsit is not here. "I smell a fight," I whisper inconspicuously to Sam and back away from the crowd.

"Don't you have any more questions for him?" she asks.

"No. He's a distraction." I look around. "This is all a big distraction. I need to think. We haven't left time for an important tip: observation, thought, and reflection. Let's go sit at the bar."

Sam parts the crowd. "Follow me."

When I fall in line with her steps, I say, "Stop scanning so much, Sam. Don't let your eyes do all the work. Tip: Look without looking."

"How?" she asks.

"Use your other senses to absorb the room around you."

Sam sucks in a breath, nods, and follows my lead. There are cheers at one table when "Blackjack" is called and jeers at another when a man yells, "Fourteen red." Nothing but useless chatter.

I lift a finger to catch the bartender's attention upon approach. "Milk. Make it a double," I say.

"Make that two doubles," Sam says.

My eyes are unfocused. I almost miss the barstool. Sam helps me up. The bartender slides two glasses of milk our way, announcing their arrival as *The Cagney Special*. I smirk until I see the young man wink at Sam.

Phlegm, phlegm, phlegm, I think to myself. Phlegm as in the calmness of temperament, not a loogie.

The bartender catches a protective-brother glare from me. "Sorry, sir," he says. "I meant no offense." He moves on to another customer.

A detective must be a steady river flowing around the case. I've never been good at this. When Billy Crust wouldn't fess up to the location of the stolen pudding cups last year, I slowly spilled his Jell-O onto his lap until he told the truth.

Sam chuckles as she sips her milk. I would almost laugh, too, if I hadn't just seen the thick makeup under the bartender's right eye. Someone's covering a black eye.

Sam spots for the bill. I tip with Bubble-Yo gum while keeping my attention on the man. When the bartender turns away, I nudge Sam, making her spill some milk. I inconspicuously tap under my right eye, nudge my head to the bartender, and gesture a punch. *He was in a fight,* I mouth.

She cocks her head and looks at the man more closely now. With pursed lips, she raps her fingers on the bar before she shouts for his attention. My eyes go wide, but it's too late to quiet her.

"Say," she drawls, more kitty than gumshoe. "What does a guy like you do around here for fun?"

The man's cheeks flush. He opens his mouth to respond.

"Number 21," I hear called out over the PA system. Sam and I exchange a sharp look. She'll have to handle the bartender on her own.

"Sam," I urgently whisper as I grip her shoulder. "Tip: Never trust deflectors. A non-answer is an answer. Something's up." I leave her with that and hurry out. It's time for my interrogation.

"Good luck," she shouts after me.

"Luck's not on my side," I say. "Facts are."

CHAPTER 32

INTERROGATION

I peek my head out of the casino's door, looking left. Cracow is talking with the couple we booted from the fake alley earlier. The security guard is nowhere to be seen. I take advantage of Cracow's distraction and hurry through the fifth and final door.

There's nothing in this room except for a wooden table and two chairs. One empty and one occupied by a demurely dressed brunette woman with brown eyes who could be none other than Libertine Justice.

The dim lighting is expected. What light there is casts striped shadows across Libertine's face from the half-open Venetian window blinds. A single light bulb dangles over her head. A bucket lamp stands beside the man dressed as an old-time police officer by the door.

"Three minutes," the officer announces. He watches the analog clock on the wall.

"Tip," I whisper to myself. "Remember: Be hard-boiled, not soft-boiled."

I've been rushing through rooms and haven't thought about what I was going to say in this interrogation. I stare at Libertine for a moment, scraping every classic movie interrogation scene to the forefront of my mind. Despite being unprepared, I throw myself into character—because if there is one thing I know, it's *Interrogation and its Everyday Uses*. My podcast trained me for this moment. I can't wait to tell my subscribers about today!

Libertine chews her lip nervously and grips the handbag on her lap with white pearl-rimmed gloves. Something feels off. It's not her nervousness. Libertine's makeup-packed face shifts slightly under my silence. Irritation. I may have seen classic movie detectives in the act a hundred times, but there is something I know just as much—1940s fashion. Libertine's appearance gives me something to work off of.

I lower my head to whisper a tip to prepare myself. "Ask the right questions. The wrong ones won't get you the right answers." I heave a slow breath, spin my Sam Spade grimace, and settle into my role.

"Nice dress, Libertine," I say and ignore her for a moment as I peel open a fresh Bubble-Yo. I don't offer her one to keep her on the edge.

She blinks at me but says nothing. I grab the lamp beside the officer and drag it to Libertine with a skin-crawling screech as the metal scratches across the floor. I place it beside her and angle the heated light on her head. Her face slacks. She knows I'm about to sweat her for the information I need, and I have about two minutes to get it.

I cross behind her and whisper a tip to myself: "Read between the lines." The person you're questioning may look like they are pausing to take a breath, but pay careful attention. They're likely working out a lie. Watch for rapid blinking or shifting eyes, possible signs that what's about to come out of their mouth is made up.

Libertine jerks to look back at me.

"A girl like you is not used to wearing wool. Are you, Ms. Justice?" I say. No response, but she tracks me with her eyes as I walk around her. A film of perspiration is already building over her thick makeup. Is it from the heat of the lamp or her cover? We'll soon see.

A bubble of excitement tickles behind my grimace. I have a chance to say a Sam Spade movie quote in a real interrogation! Casually, I spit out his exact words from *The Maltese Falcon*. "You, uh, you aren't exactly the sort of person you pretend to be. Are ya?"

She sputters. "What do you mean?" Not the follow-up line I was hoping for but close enough.

I drive in Spade's words, so they hit home. "The schoolgirl manner. You know, blushing, stammering, and all that."

Libertine says nothing. I say it for her. "I've seen your place," I continue, impressed with my tone. "Silk seems more your type."

"What are you talking about?" She's fishing for innocence and coming up short.

"Don't play innocent with me." I slam my hands down on the table and chomp on my gum like a camel eating. I soften my hard edge and whisper to her, "Mauve won't cover your story."

"Who's Mauve?" She lifts one brow with a skill that tells me she does it often.

"Not *who* . . ." I nudge my head to her dull coat and snap my gum in my mouth. "But *what*. The color *mauve*. It doesn't match all the makeup you've caked on."

The heat is working. Libertine unlatches the high neck of her coat. I cock my head at the string around her neck that is visible for a blink. Could it be a string to hide something small enough to fit on a key ring?

It's mine, Libertine Justice, the letter said.

"One minute left," the officer calls out.

My partner's words hit me: *If the envelope wasn't addressed to Libertine, the way the letter is written, it looks like it was signed by her.* I don't skip a beat. I fumble in my pocket for my field notebook and pen. "Ms. Justice, can you sign your name for me?"

"What for?" she says sharply. A layer of virtue has peeled away. She's built for the art of being deceptively vulnerable and wickedly deceitful.

"The guys bet me I wouldn't get to talk to the beautiful Libertine Justice. They'd never believe me." I glance at the clock. Fifteen seconds to lift off.

She hesitates, grabs the pen I have extended to her, and signs my notebook. In a beat of her finishing, I slap the letter from her apartment on the table. The signatures match. *Boom, blast off.* I grin hard.

"It was yours," I say. "And now *it's mine,* Libertine Justice. Hand over what's around your neck, or I'll have the officer do it for you."

Libertine starts to cry as she unties the string. "You're making a terrible mistake."

I flap my hand like I don't care. I don't have time for her act. "Hand it over."

She pulls the string free from her coat. A key dangles from the end of it. I snatch it and charge out the door, ignoring her incessant shouts about the terrible mistake I'm making.

Libertine's cries have caught the attention of contestants in the hallway. Sam is gaping at me as I storm through the door with the key in my hand. People gasp and murmur. They can calm down. This isn't over. My chase for the Maltese Falcon trophy has just begun.

CHAPTER 33

CRACOW

I stand in front of Cracow's desk and look him in the eye—slightly peeved I'm too short to look down at him while he's sitting. His eyes grow hungry at the sight of the key. The look halts my hand, and instead, I shove the key into my pocket. Interesting. With the other hand, I pull out the small Plexiglas box with the egg timer and slam it on his desk. Three minutes left on the clock. Excited cheers roar behind me.

"This is not the Great Whatsit," I say steadily to Cracow. "But it means something, and I don't intend to waste my time." I rap my fingers on the box.

Cracow glowers. "It means double the prize if you locate the real Great Whatsit before the fake bomb goes off." He flashes a snarl. "Tick tock."

My breath catches, but I hold my glare. $2,000 for winning. I'll have a thousand bucks for Mom after I split the money with Sam.

Cracow taps a fist on his desk, moving my focus to his hand and his bruised knuckles. My mind deduces this case with rapid-fire speed— kicking away irrelevant pieces and snapping others together like a master brick builder.

I glance back at Sam whose face is scrunched with worry. My heart jolts at the sight of the large security guard walking out of the apartment at the end of the hall. Tick tock, indeed.

"That's right, kid," Cracow whispers, following my stare. "You're not supposed to be here, are you?" An EXIT sign blazes in the dark hallway casting Cracow with a red hue.

My brows pulse together. Why would he say that? The timer ticks and ticks, challenging my heart with its pace. No time.

"I—I'm his guardian," Sam says, pushing forward. "Keep going, Marlowe!"

I straighten my back and lift my chin, sliding my hand along the brim of my hat. "I'm exactly where I need to be, Cracow." I'm here to win.

I've always trusted my gut. Facts are facts. There are some holes in this investigation, but I know one thing's for sure—a bruised right fist matches a bruised right eye, and together, they can make a broken cabinet.

At this moment, nothing else exists. No mom, no grandpa, no money, no emotions. No Maltese Falcon trophy. It's just Cracow and me. "You had a scuffle. Didn't you?" I ask.

Cracow's jaw clenches.

"Bad temper? The bruising on your knuckles is too bright to be from when you punched through your garage wall last month." The last part was a wild pitch, but the shift of his eyes tells me I found the catcher's mitt. I pull the key out of my pocket and dangle it in front of him. "Is this why Libertine won't see you?"

Cracow snaps to his feet, too steady for a man with a cane. More puzzle pieces click together. People behind me hoot. I stroll to the side of his desk with a glance at the egg timer. "You have a few of these keys. Don't you? Libertine stole hers back from off your key ring. You didn't like that. Did you?" My talk is quick and punchy. Still no answer from Cracow, but he grinds his teeth. Answers aren't always words.

I keep spitting out the facts as they line up. "That wasn't you in the alley yesterday arguing with Libertine. It was the bartender. The bartender you fought last night in the casino because you thought he had this key. But he didn't because yesterday he still thought you had it. The bartender covered his bruised eye to keep his job. He needs the money. So, he's not someone who would have a flashy car. No, no. It's your garage, your key ring. You're the collector." *Snap, snap*, I hear in my head as I deduce the snot out of this stuffy case.

I sigh, despite the dwindling time. I'll need to include a tip about making time on your side in my essay. "See," I continue, "this key was not yours or the bartender's. It belonged to Libertine. She sent herself a letter to claim it as her own in case anything happened to her. Libertine needs this key more than you or the bartender." My voice trails off with my thoughts. The answer is right there at the tip of my tongue. *The key is to something . . .* I think. *Something she gives and takes away.*

Grandpa Gilbert's words about the Great Whatsit returns: *Its existence was simply a fact, not something they could hold.*

The key is to something that can't be held.

I let out a long breath and lower my head to sift through the last clues. What can a person give and take away? My eyes catch on what is perceived to be Cracow's injured left leg—and spot where the fabric of his trousers clings to a bulge on his shin. *Snap* goes the last piece of the puzzle.

"Is the key the Great Whatsit?" shouts an overly eager onlooker.

I shake my head. I've always trusted my gut, but that doesn't mean it has always been right. I have no choice now. It's like in the movies when a character must choose between cutting the red or the blue wire to stop a bomb. *Red wire. Blue wire.* I make my choice.

I snatch the cane nearby and whack Cracow's shin. He grunts. There are surprised gasps from the crowd, and then silence as a tin container falls down Cracow's pant leg and clatters at his feet. I snatch it before he can grab it. I hold up a red heart-shaped tin with a keyhole to the crowd. *Gut, I owe you a sundae*, I think. All the puzzle pieces are now together. Confidence pushes me on. Clever producers.

"*Love*," I announce. "Love is what Cracow collects, and the innocent bartender was desperate for. Love is what Libertine Justice shares and steals back from men to fund her lifestyle. Love is the Great Whatsit."

I shove the tin and key into Sam's hands when the security guard reaches the crowd. "Find me where the Maltese Falcon plays," I whisper to her intensely as I back away. Sam's clever. She'll know I mean the movie. I need that money, but I can't stay any longer. They know I'm not supposed to be here. Sam could get in trouble for covering for me.

"Cracow," I call out. "You're ordered to pay restitution to Libertine Justice." I've always wanted to say that. Cracow reaches for me. I snake by. The timer buzzes, but I'm already plowing through the exit door.

CHAPTER 34

THE CHASE

My heart pounding in my ears blocks out the cheering behind me. My heavy breathing echoes off the walls. This is a thousand dreams and nightmares coming to life in one wild sprint. I run as footsteps thunder behind me.

The door labeled EXIT wasn't the actual exit. It took me to another long hallway. At the end of it, I kick my way out of the convention hall. I grip my hat and wince into the afternoon sun. It's close to 2:30 p.m. *The Maltese Falcon* film is starting soon. I need to get to the East Theater, where they're playing movies, to meet Sam and collect the winnings, but someone's hot on my tail.

My instincts were right. Security had its eyes on me. Maybe they found out I've been lying about not being alone. I have no time to be cornered for questioning. The adrenaline I get after a case is solved pushes me on.

The exit booted me into a real alley filled with real trash and grime. There's even a stray Chihuahua dog. Commotion barrels through the hallway.

I try to catch my breath. "Alone . . . in an alley . . . is a good time . . . to call for backup." But I have no one I can call.

I take off down the alley toward the street. Now, I have a Chihuahua nipping at my heels too. A door crashes open. I look back. The security guard shouts. The Chihuahua yelps.

"Tip: It's okay . . . to be afraid. Just don't . . . show it." I pick up speed, look forward, and scream.

At the end of the alley, a taxicab blocks me in. I slam against it. The number sixteen has never looked so sweet.

"Get in," Ben says.

Tip: Watch your . . . butt. I dive onto the back seat as the Chihuahua dives for me. I get the door closed in time. Ben drives off slowly like I'm a regular pickup. He circles the block in silence. With gulping breaths, I glance over my shoulder a few times. When I know I'm safe, I rest my head back.

On the second lap of the block, Ben finally says, "I wouldn't have guessed you to be one to stiff a man."

I swallow and wipe the sweat from my face. He doesn't say anything else. It's enough to make me feel terrible. I lower my head.

"Did you get your Maltese Falcon trophy?" he asks after letting his silent reprimand burn me long enough.

I shake my head, holding my frown. "Not exactly." I pull my pocket watch out. "I need to collect it in five minutes." My lips tilt into a pout. How am I going to get back in to find Sam? I should call my mom soon, but I don't want to do it until I have the money.

"What have you been up to?"

"Acting like I've got nothing to do and a lot of time to do it," I say. My words sound like a deflating balloon. I mumble to my pocket, "Insert tip."

Ben's eyes narrow. He pulls over and gets out. My brows pinch as I watch him walk around the taxicab and open my door. He waves a hand.

I slouch. "Are you kicking me out?"

"No, I'm babysitting."

"Wait. You'll get me back in?" My voice cracks.

Ben nods curtly.

"But . . ." I say with a fresh frown. "I think the security guards know I snuck in without a guardian. They won't let me in again."

"They will if you're with me. Get out, kid."

"You don't have to ask me twice." I slide along the back seat and jump out. Sam could be looking for me right now. I need to find her. "Ben, you can't park here."

"A taxi driver can park anywhere."

As we walk to the festival, I say, "I'll pay you for all your troubles. I swear it."

He puts an arm across my shoulders and replies, "I'm getting paid, kid. Don't worry about it."

Security is distracted when we breeze past them. No one pays us attention as we enter the East Gate to the theater. Sam is nowhere in sight. What if they don't give the winnings to her because I'm not there? What if she takes it all?

Ben grins at the Sam Spade poster by the theater. "Is this your Maltese Falcon trophy?"

I'm about to tell him the truth, but instead, I sigh at the light that glows on the old man's face seeing the poster. "Yeah," I reply with a smirk. "Yeah, this is the Maltese Falcon I'm looking for. Can I treat you to a movie?"

"I'd like that," he replies.

I shouldn't be going to the movie. I should find Sam. But the look on Ben's face, everything he's done for me, I can't ditch him now.

Inside the theater, the sight of the big screen has shaken every worry away. Mom searching for me, the money lost, getting to Florida—they can wait for one hour and forty-one minutes before crashing in on me. For now, I'm safe. Sam Spade's here . . . and Ben too.

Ben checks his phone and shoves it in his pocket before taking a seat at my left. I got lucky with an aisle seat.

As the lights dim, I bounce on my heels, which I'm sitting on to see better. I find my smile when I look at Ben, and for the first time, he smiles back.

"Kid," Ben says.

"Yeah," I whisper excitedly.

"The second you start quoting lines during the movie, I'm out of here."

It's too dark for him to see, but I frown. "*Fine*." I pause and grin. "But this is the stuff that dreams are made of."

Ben chuckles at how I snuck in the last line of the movie. "That's all you get," he says. And I'm all right with that.

We settle in and watch the movie on the silver screen as it is meant to be seen. "Tip," I murmur when I remember my recorder is still on. "Dream big. Life just might spit a drop of opportunity on you." I finally turn my recorder off.

CHAPTER 35

MOM

My face is beaming when the movie ends. I didn't want it to stop, but I'm happy to have lived it. As Ben and I leave our seats, I chat nonstop about fun facts from the movie.

"The three props used as the Maltese Falcon in the movie are valued at over a million dollars now. I made one once out of a cheese block for a school project. I kept it until mold swallowed it up. Humphrey Bogart had to supply his own wardrobe for the movie. So his style is completely authentic, not manufactured."

Ben simply pats my back and lets me talk. I burst out of the theater into the lobby, and all joy shrivels up into a tight ball of frozen terror.

Mom. My mom, Freyda Plum, is waiting. Her name badge is still pinned to her uniform. A wild sob pinches her face when she sees me walk out. Her fists clench. Her cheeks puff like they do when she is so angry she can't speak. Security guards are with her. They keep their distance, likely as terrified as I am.

Know when to roll credits. This day is done. I push up the brim of my hat. "Ben, you're going to have to help me with this one," I whisper through my strained smile. No response. I look over my shoulder. The people leaving the theater push past. Ben is gone.

"Icabum Plum!" my mom says. Her voice is shrill, like a Pterodactyl's cry. Unlucky for everyone standing nearby, Mom has found her voice again. "Come here, *right now.*"

Oh, boy. I raise my surrendering hands. "Tip," I whisper to the air. "You are protected from the enormity of your stupidity—for a time." Dang. My recorder's off. No quick moves. Not with the scary face Mom is making. I search for Sam, but she and my $1,000 are probably long gone. "Mom, I can explain—"

"No. You are going to sit on this bench and listen to the sheer terror I felt when I couldn't find you." Tears are making Mom messy, and she doesn't care. When she's in full parent mode, nothing gets in the way. Not even self-control. I sit and wince every time her voice pitches. People rush past in fear Medusa might turn her wrath on them. The security guards stay silent, but even they flinch a few times.

"The bus driver and the nice lady I had looking after you called me right away. They said you ran off! Why?"

I stay silent because the question is rhetorical. She knows why if she's standing here. Looking back, I'm not surprised Vito and the crazy lady from the bus were in Mom's crew. An oversight because I was distracted with getting to the film festival. I settle into my slouch. The weight of her disappointment pulls my chest to the ground. I knew we'd be having this talk. I didn't think it'd be so soon.

Mom has been hunting me most of the day which means she missed work, lost wages, and gathered who knows what repercussions from her boss, Big Herb. This day is costing her more than a few tears. I don't even have the winnings to cushion the blow. My foot bounces. I shouldn't have come here today. That's saying something about how sucky I feel.

"*And then,*" she says, her voice deep and demonic to match her look. "I get a call from Farney Fig around one o'clock saying some man called your work looking for *me* and said you were hours away alone at a film festival. Your school called too. They received the same message for me!"

My face slacks. Ben. I drew him a straight line to Circle's End with my school's phone number and the business card to my work. Ben sent out an alert to find my mom since I stiffed him in giving her number. I glance around. Where did Ben go?

"*Oh no!* You look at me, Icky."

I do as she says and recoil when I stare into the inferno.

"Sheriff has a command station set up for information on your whereabouts." She makes a feral growl when I give an impressed frown over the effort. "Our whole town has shut down to help look for you."

Dang. The most exciting case to happen to my boring town and I missed it.

"Sheriff called here once we found out where you were while I drove his truck like a maniac to get you. These nice security guards have been trying to track you down. Now start talking." She stares at me all wild-eyed. I consider holding up my hands in case her eyes pop out.

"I thought I could win the contest money to help you with the bills," I mumble and then try to will Sam to show up with the winnings.

The rain cloud is over me. I feel like a sad, soaked Humphrey Bogart in *Casablanca* when he's waiting in the rain at the train station for Ingrid Bergman to arrive. She doesn't, but he gets a note. I don't even get that.

"Nothing is worth the risk of losing you, Icky. Nothing." She's sobbing hard. I should hug her, but I'm frozen with shame. "Why couldn't you just stay on bus #32?"

"*Because,*" I say a little too sharply. The flint to my shame sparks with fire.

Mom's head jerks back like she's been slapped. I never talk to her like that, but she hit a wound I'd sewn up since the *Dad* case. My heel bounces faster. A snarl flickers as I hold back the anger that is threatening tears. It gets worse when Mom's soggy face softens with understanding.

"Your dad is very worried—"

"So why isn't *he* here?" Sadness tightens my throat and my voice cracks. "Tell me what he said to you when he found out I was missing."

Mom's eyes are strained. She shakes her head.

I roll my eyes with a sniff of my nose. "Don't hide it from me."

Mom's shoulders sink. She dips her head. After a pause, she replies, "I couldn't get ahold of him. I talked to Betty before she left for the depot to pick you up."

I snort a laugh. "I knew it."

"Is this all to get his attention?" Mom asks. "He wants to spend time with you."

"No. I don't want his attention. And he only wants to spend his time his way and make me like him. Dad doesn't even know me and doesn't want to get to know me."

"Have you ever told him that?"

"Has he ever called to chat?" I know my tone is gruff and rude, but something is bleeding out of me, and too many people can see it. I yank my hat lower over my burning face.

Mom has found some composure and settles next to me on the bench with a sigh. "I wish I knew how you felt before all this."

I've never wanted to burden her before. My emotions are locked away not only because of my job as a detective but because of my mom. I have to be strong for her. She's done everything for me. Why weigh her down with something that she has no control over? My dad left her the same as he left me.

Mom picks at her thumb as she thinks for a moment. "You're old enough now to control your relationship with your dad." I tilt my head to see her. She grips my knee. "See him if you want to. Don't if you don't. But to be in control, you have to do something first."

"What's that?" I mumble and taste tears.

"By the end of the week, you have to write everything you've ever wanted to tell him down on paper. That means looking inside yourself and figuring out what bothers you most."

Great another essay. "What do I do with the paper?"

"Mail it to him if you want to. Or not. But you will feel better after you write it. You hold everything in. It's not good."

She's right. It's not good. Doom and gloom are what I'll find if I open up that locker. But I don't need to worry about tapping into that darkness just yet. "I don't have to see Dad right now if I agree to write the letter?"

She nods. A smile plays on her sad face. "When you're back from grandma and grandpa's, I want to see that you've done it."

My eyelids snap wide. I sit up straight. "G—grandma and grandpa's?" Through the chaos of the last hour, I'd forgotten. Enzo is already in Florida!

Mom smacks tears from her face, further smearing her mascara. "Grandpa called. I was hysterical after talking to your work and school. When I told him where I was headed to get you, Grandpa asked if you could go to visit him after. He's not supposed to push himself too hard, but he was excited to set up his fishing boat for the three of you." Her brows scrunch. "I don't know how he got Grandma to agree to go fishing."

My eyes practically bulge out of their sockets. Grandma Ginger will not set foot on a boat! Enzo must have gone to see Grandpa and the old man is covering for him . . . for me. I nod eagerly.

"I told him no way and that you were infinitely grounded, but . . ." She heaves a sigh. "I don't stand a chance against Grandpa when it comes to you." I'm sitting so straight I could be a show dog trying to earn every point I can get.

Mom kisses my cheek and stands, crossing her arms tightly over her chest as she does. Her eyes narrow as she turns to look down at me. She could be a shapeshifter for how quickly she can transform her face with her moods. "We are not done." Any excitement fizzles like a hot pan without bacon. "You are grounded until May 1."

"But—" I catch my retort. Seventeen days in the can. She's not unreasonable, but it stings.

"Now, the matter of you getting to Florida. You're not old enough to take the train by yourself—"

"I have an ID that says I am."

I try to spin an easy smile, but it turns mushy when she yells, "What!" Mom looks to the sky with a pinched-eyed prayer.

I get up and hug her as tightly as I can. Her chest rumbles with her cry. I should have hugged her right away. It's what she needed.

"I know it isn't enough right now," I say, "but I'm sorry."

"I don't know what I would do if I lost you," she says against my head.

Tears prick at my eyes. "I love you too."

I hear shouts. My name carries across the empty lobby. "Marlowe!"

CHAPTER 36

MALTESE FALCON

I look past Mom and see Sam jogging over to me. My mouth drops open. "Oh, thank heavens," she says as I hurry to meet her halfway. Mom follows behind me. "You said to find you where the Maltese Falcon plays, but I never saw you enter the theater. I thought you left."

"Only my dignity left," I reply. Mom looks between Sam and me with pursed lips. "Mom," I say. "This is Sam."

Sam blushes. "Actually, it's Aniyah. Sam is always my alias when I work the film festival."

"You work here?" I check my voice level and see the bartender stroll up after her.

"Yeah. My boyfriend Miguel and I love classic movies and follow this festival."

"Well, you make a good partner," I say.

Aniyah gives my shoulder a friendly nudge.

"If you're ever in Circle's End, I have a few friends I'd like you to meet." She will be the Gum Chews' first honorary member.

Aniyah grins and nods. "Kid, we've been working this festival for three years, and I've never seen anyone solve the featured case as fast as you did. They even made it extra hard this time."

My cheeks heat. "It was no big deal," I reply.

Mom rubs my back, but her scrunched face tells me she's totally lost.

"No big deal?" Aniyah snorts and pulls out an envelope from her back pocket. The word *WINNER* is written on it. I recognize Libertine Justice's handwriting. "Your winnings. $1,000. Plus, a $1,000 bonus for beating the clock. Our deal doesn't count since I work here. So, it's all yours."

The words slowly swirl around me until they slap my face. I stumble as they sink in. Mom puts her hands over her gasp.

"And Mom?" Aniyah adds while unfolding a piece of paper. "If you can quickly sign this consent form while no one is looking, we'll pretend you were here all along." There is a heart-stopping pause while Mom considers contributing to my transgression. I release a breath when she signs.

"Oh! *And* . . ." Aniyah reaches into her satchel and pulls out a small, glistening-black plastic statue. I squeal as she sets the Maltese Falcon in my shaking hands. "Everyone's talking about you in Mystery Hall, kid. You earned this."

My mouth unhinges, and it sounds like I'm choking. The shape of the black plastic bird modeled after the movie is exact. Aniyah passes the money to Mom. I forget all partner formalities and dive in to hug Aniyah.

When I break away, she says, "Do you think you can make it next year?" Her voice settles into uncertainty when she looks at my mom's crazy-mom face.

Mom answers for me. "How about I give you my phone number, and you can call *me* with the details?"

I grip her waist with a super hug.

"I haven't promised anything," Mom says. "Let's see how good you are this year."

I release her from my clutches. "I'll be good. I promise," I reply, with my fingers crossed behind my back. I give Aniyah a wink. Tip: Every detective carries his or her own definition of good.

CHAPTER 37

TWENTY BOGARTS

Fake Frank Sinatra saves the day. The famous singer once known as Ol' Blue Eyes snatches Mom's mood and fills it like a helium balloon. The man singing the hits in Mystery Hall may go by Phil from Milwaukee when his shift is up, but he is the real deal to Mom. She soars to the moon, nearly forgetting how angry she is at me. Nearly.

Mom rarely gets a break from work. She is always picking up double shifts. I'm glad the contest winnings will help. She works hard to give me the things she thinks I need to keep me on the right path in life. For fifteen minutes on the dance floor, I show her all I need is my mother.

When my awkwardly stiff dance solo is over, I reach into my pocket for my recorder. "Tip: Keep a smart lady in your life. And listen to her."

My smile is the fullest it's been in a long time when I leave the Galagala Convention Center holding my Maltese Falcon trophy. Mom snaps a photo of me with twenty Bogart impersonators. I text the picture to Enzo. He replies right away with a wide-eyed emoji face. I can't wait to hear about his trip to Florida with Artie and Paoula. Reuniting with my best friend will be like Peter Pan finding his shadow again. I'm kissing my lucky stars that he didn't get in trouble. I know Mom suspects I had help, but she can't prove it.

Sheriff loaned Mom his truck. I'm excited to ride in it, but the thrill fizzles when Mom tosses a warning that I can't touch any buttons, especially not the two-way radio. When I see what's on my seat, I freeze.

"Oh, sorry," she says. "Move those squash to the ground. Sheriff picked them up at Greta's house when he was asking around town about you."

That Sheriff is a good man, I think with a chuckle. When I jump onto the seat, Mom hands me a heavy plastic bag.

"I went by the Chokeberrys looking for you," she says as she gets behind the wheel. "Your friends helped set up the command station in the town hall. When I was leaving to come find you, Tyler wanted me to give you that care package."

From the outside, the clear plastic bag that the brothers drew hearts on looks to be filled with all sorts of snacks. But I know better. The funny sayings on the bag and the pile of candy are distractions from the two Altoids containers clinking on the bottom.

"They are nice boys," Mom says as she drives off.

I hold the bag close to me and smile. "Some of the best out there."

The whole way to the train station, I search for taxis, hoping to spot Ben's number 16. A thank you to the taxi driver wouldn't be enough. I hope he'll find his way through Circle's End one day and look me up. I owe him a proper tip.

CHAPTER 38

TRAINED EYE

om told the train conductor, a crewmember, and the family next to where she found me a seat on the train to keep an eye on her *twelve-year-old son*. She risked perjury to take her chances with me on a train. However, it earned me an extra day of grounding for the fake ID.

It feels more like a prison train. And like a prison, I have time. Lots and lots of time. Station Eighteen can't come fast enough. I dig through my bag from the Chokeberrys and go right for the containers at the bottom. I pull both out. The first one I open has a tightly rolled charger and earbuds. The second one is a new walkie with a fresh battery. Tyler's engineering skills are getting better, or his father had a hand in it. This new design looks more legit with its polished interior. It even has a plug for headsets to be discreet.

I plug in the headsets and put the buds in my ears. I tuck the container into my pocket. The simple movement makes my jail-guardians wary of me. The middle-aged couple in bright-colored vacation clothes shifts their bottoms. They sit facing me in our group of seats. Their legs are trapped within a pile of baby stuff. The man adjusts the sleeping baby on his lap. I sigh. Mom should have been a politician. She can wrangle anyone to her side. I give the family a strained smile.

"I need to make a phone call." I whisper the words so as to seem courteous and not wake up their baby. I push the button on the walkie headset cord and let out a whistle.

A pause, a *click*, and a series of clunks as the Chokeberrys fight to get to their walkie.

"Ick!" they scream in unison.

"Hey, gentlemen," I reply with a grin. "Thanks for the care package. Over."

"Good to hear from you," says Tyrone. "How much trouble are you in? Over."

"A reasonable amount. But I'm allowed to go to my grandparents and meet up with Enzo. I'm on a train heading there now. Over."

Excited hoots follow. "Things were pretty crazy here while everyone looked for you," Tyrone says. "I hope it was worth it. Did you win? Over."

I shift in my seat. A frown tugs at my lips. "Yeah. I got my Maltese Falcon trophy. Over."

"Sweet!"

"And I won $2,000. Over."

"No way!"

"The money will help my mom, but today may have caused some trouble with Big Herb. Over." I scratch at a spot on my trousers. The Chokeberrys are well aware of my archnemesis.

"Ick, it's Tyler. About that, I've had a . . . breakthrough on Project B I'd like to show you when you're back. Find me at school. I think you will be pleased with how it's progressing. Over."

A smile fills my face. Project B. *B* for *Big Herb*. "Excellent. I trust this with no one else. Over."

"Except me, right?" Tyrone jumps in with his loud, boisterous voice. "It's sort of a package deal."

I chuckle. "Yes. Is Enzo on? Over." Enzo won't jump into a conversation. He waits to be invited in.

"Ten-four, 'lil buddy. Over," shouts the voice of an older man.

"Grandpa!"

"Yep. Enzo's here too. Showed up on my doorstep like a lost puppy." Grandpa Gilbert gives a thick cough. "Boy, you're in a heap of trouble. Sorry, I couldn't be there too. Can't wait to hear all about it."

"Grandpa," Tyrone butts in. "You're supposed to say *over*—"

Tyler shushes him.

"I'm excited to see you," I say. "Thanks to everyone listening. I better go. Tyler's walkie battery is terrible. Over."

"Well, now you have the battery charger!" Tyler says.

I laugh. "Over and out."

I lean my head back against the seat and take a calming breath. Good friends, good family. Sometimes, I focus too much on the bad things that have shaped me, and I forget all the good in my life that makes me better every day.

My dad doesn't deserve a whole essay from me pouring my guts out over what I hate or what makes me mad. Instead, he will get a short message with all he's missing out on.

I'll write: *My name is Icabum Plum. Son of the toughest lady I know. I have a best friend I love fishing with. I'm a part-time straight-A student and a full-time detective. I dress the way I do because it makes me feel good. I use old movies to teach me how to be tough and smart, but the real lessons come from my mom. I've made myself the person I am—and it's as normal as I get.*

Done. Easier than I thought when I focus on the positive. Now, I can move on.

I plug my earbuds into my recorder and rewind the day back to the very beginning. Mom's now-crumpled note she wanted me to use for the women's restroom falls out of my pocket when I remove my field notebook. *I give my son permission to be in here–Freyda Plum*, it says.

I chuckle a weary sound. I could have used this permission slip all along. The note gets tucked back in my pocket for another day.

I get to work jotting down and organizing my tips as I hear them. I even add a few tips that I wish I had remembered while I was working on the case. I turn off the recorder for a break and rub my fingers in my eyes. Wonderwood Station is announced. I feel a tug on my chest when the train lets up speed. Two more hours in this compartment.

The sun has set. Its last rays stretch the shadows of travelers walking along the station's platform. My eyes roam around the people in the compartment.

Tip, I write. *Training is never over.*

Across the aisle: A woman on the other side of my jail-guardians. She smelled nice when I stood behind her getting on the train. Brown eyes: Unfocused. Thoughtful? Tired? Right hand: wrinkled, worn, resting precariously on the strap of her open purse that dangles off her seat.

I keep going. My sight drifts to a man with his back to the lovely-smelling woman. Right hand: Fingers are thin and long like spider legs, itching his thigh slowly. A sign of anxious thoughts? Green eyes: Focused down at his side. Focused where? I follow his stare. He coughs. I look back at him with a raised brow. His hand drops to what he's been watching.

"Ma'am?" I say. The jail-guardians stir. A few women look my way, but not the one I want. "Ma'am?" I say louder. "Your purse is open."

The woman I'd been observing blinks and turns to me. I point at her purse. She blinks again, looks down, and jolts forward to pull the bag to her side. She nods a thank you. I glance behind her and find the green-eyed man staring at me. He gets up with a stretch and looks down at me before heading out of our compartment. My nose starts to itch.

I can never ignore the itch. Even now, with Mom trying her trust in me once more.

I scratch at my knee and eye the jail-guardians. They have my luggage above their heads where Mom asked them to watch it. The baby on the man's lap is fast asleep. No parent would want to wake a sleeping baby on a train.

I gag once, twice, thrice.

"You okay, Icabum," my female guard worriedly asks.

"I'm—" I gag again. "I knew I shouldn't have gone for the curry hot-dog." I jump to my feet. The male guard's eyes strain because he can't get up. The woman is not able to get around him.

"Be right back." My words are muffled behind my hand.

I sprint a few steps out of their view and then saunter the rest of the way, lowering my fedora hat over my brows. The compartment rumbles beneath my feet with the feel of the railroad tracks. The squeal of metal on metal burns my ears as the train slows to a stop. At the door that divides the compartments, I lift to my toes to look through the window. The green-eyed man sits behind another woman. His hand expertly slips into her purse and slides out with her wallet. I flash my teeth. Once again, my senses are spot on. This skill is a blessing and a curse.

He's up and moving in a blink, gaining speed. I kick open the door and start running, shouting the crime as I fly by passengers. The man is off the train, fading into the crowd on the platform. The train's horn toots a warning. There's no thought about consequences when justice needs to be served. I turn on my recorder.

"Tip: A good detective never turns off. There is no peace for those trying to keep the peace." I leap off the train.

Case closed.

One Hundred Ways to Be a Gum Chew with Gumption:
The Unofficial Guide for Unsanctioned Detectives Doing Unauthorized Work

AN ESSAY BY ICABUM PLUM

I'll never wear a cape, but maybe one day, I'll wear a badge. Keeping this town, my chunk of the world, safe is a gritty job, but I'm a detective up for the challenge. I'm the eyes behind heads, the gum sticking to shoes, a shifting shadow on a summer stroll. When I'm seen, it's too late for someone on the wrong side of the law. With my training guide, you will learn the skills to join me. Together, we will make our world a better place.

Golden Rules

These top ten tips create a firm foundation for the other guidelines. Get them right, and you will be one step up from a detective Scooby-Doo cartoon and a haircut away from a *Hardy Boys* novel.

- **Tip 1:** Know yourself before you can begin to understand others. Essential advice I learned over spring break from a wise taxi driver named Ben. Play-Doh is nothing without a mold. Establish what your frame looks like, and you are well on your way.

- **Tip 2:** Get a partner. Someone to have your back and keep you on track.

- **Tip 3:** Answers are in the details. Don't search puzzle pieces by shape. Look at the images on the parts.

- **Tip 4:** Observation, thought, and reflection. Let it be your mantra.

- **Tip 5:** Phlegm. Not the loogie, but the calmness of temperament. It is harder to see a stick in a rapid stream. Settle your mind, slow your flow, and see clearer.

- **Tip 6:** Look without looking. Enlist your other senses. Staring directly at a culprit will blow your surveillance.

- **Tip 7:** Allow time to think. Every day, we absorb countless amounts of information. Find a quiet space to let the data settle in.

- **Tip 8:** Determination. It's the gas in a detective's tank.

- **Tip 9:** Dress the part. Wear the clothes of the person you want to be. If it looks like a banana and acts like a banana, then it is a banana. More on this later—the clothes, not bananas.

- **Tip 10:** Be a Renaissance type—a jack of all trades and master of none. Or master all and rule the world. Don't let me hold you back. This is a good segue into the next topic, *Skill Development.*

Skill Development

Detective skills need conditioning, and mine stay well-oiled. If not, I'll get rusty. Let the following thirty-five tips dangle at the back of your mind. The more you build them, the more familiar they feel—like braces. They are put in place for improvement.

- **Tip 11:** Strengthen your memory. The mind is a detective's greatest tool.

- **Tip 12:** Be a life hacker. Understand your resources so they may be used to your advantage.

- **Tip 13:** The power of deduction is strengthened with logic and critical thinking.

- **Tip 14:** Read between the lines. Dig for the hidden meaning behind what someone says or does.

- **Tip 15:** Quick talk. Tangle your suspect with words.

- **Tip 16:** Don't move your lips when you speak. Keep the focus on your eyes, not your words.

- **Tip 17:** Organize the scene yourself. Don't see the same way others see.

- **Tip 18:** Reconstruct the events of the crime. Follow how the dominoes fell.

- **Tip 19:** See from another perspective. Consider bird's eye and worm views.

- **Tip 20:** Interview in a group to watch reactions. People relax when they aren't in the hot seat.

- **Tip 21:** Make time on your side by not wasting it.

- **Tip 22:** Believe your instincts. Primal reactions are programmed into our DNA.

- **Tip 23:** There's always more than one way to get an answer. Don't give up too quickly.

- **Tip 24:** Ask the right questions. The wrong ones won't get you the right answer.

- **Tip 25:** Fighting is overrated. Your quick wit will get you out of a situation much faster.

- **Tip 26:** Master the slap. If you must fight, a quick slap will stun your opponent long enough for you to get away.

- **Tip 27:** Be the part you are playing. Banana, banana, banana.

- **Tip 28:** Learn to sketch, in case you don't have a camera.

- **Tip 29:** Use code words. Puns, gestures, Pig Latin, quotes. Find a style that best fits you.

- **Tip 30:** Know when to shut up. Silence is powerful.

- **Tip 31:** Understand how long to boil an egg. There's a point where everyone cracks.

- **Tip 32:** Identify when the goose is cooked, meaning know your limits.

- **Tip 33:** Be careful, not careless. (Source: Freyda Plum)

- **Tip 34:** Do your research. Homework is not just a school thing. It is a life thing. Get used to it.

- **Tip 35:** Know the difference between punditry and pungency. One makes you wiser.

- **Tip 36:** Choose a skill for distraction. Something to divert suspicion, like magic.

- **Tip 37:** Footprints at a scene are one thing, but the area around the footprints is more telling.

- **Tip 38:** Neat note-taking. Ugly writing helps no one.

- **Tip 39:** Flawless filing. Keep your cases well organized for easy reference.

- **Tip 40:** Scrupulousness. A big word about little things. Attention to detail is important.

- **Tip 41:** Craft your disguises. If a popper is trying to be a prince, wear the tights.

- **Tip 42:** Feathered feet, not giant stomps. Ballet classes have helped me.

- **Tip 43:** Sight is an infinite amount of details. Wade through it to find what is out of place.

- **Tip 44:** Crime will enlist all your senses. Don't rely only on what you see.

- **Tip 45:** Fast-talking is your job. Stop the jabber-mouth suspect from the start. You set the pace.

Thirty Warnings to Remember

The following is a list of warnings, all confirmed in the field by yours truly. Detectives are allowed to make mistakes. Contrary to popular belief, we are human, too.

- **Tip 46:** Cases will find you, so be ready. Always carry a travel kit of necessities.

- **Tip 47:** Don't forget federal, local, and natural laws apply to you.

- **Tip 48:** Survival is your will to survive. Never give up on yourself.

- **Tip 49:** Try to be honest, but always be ethical.

- **Tip 50:** Don't forget to eat. Nothing too heavy, or else a tempered stomach might spoil your case.

- **Tip 51:** Choose a comfort fidget to redirect your emotions so they don't show on your face.

- **Tip 52:** Beware of ennui. Ennui is boredom caused by a lack of interest, and it will hinder motivation.

- **Tip 53:** Never trust deflectors. A non-answer is an answer. Something's up.

- **Tip 54:** It's okay to call for backup.

- **Tip 55:** Everyone's a suspect. (Source: Aniyah, honorary Gum Chew)

- **Tip 56:** Truth hurts, but it's the truth.

- **Tip 57:** Constant reasoning and thinking allow little time for sleep.

- **Tip 58:** Pick up random facts like pennies. You never know when you'll need one.

- **Tip 59:** You are protected from the enormity of your stupidity for a time.

- **Tip 60:** Gumshoes don't go on holidays. They go on breaks.

- **Tip 61:** Death-stick cigarettes aren't a fashion worth reviving, like sunbathing and hitchhiking.

- **Tip 62:** Keep a smart lady in your life.

- **Tip 63:** One step back can be better than running two steps forward.

- **Tip 64:** Keep a steady moral compass.

- **Tip 65:** Trust is like your heart. Don't give it willingly. (Source: Ben from taxicab #16)

- **Tip 66:** Watch your butt. Glance behind you when you're charging forward.

- **Tip 67:** Cause & correlation. One doesn't always mean the other.

- **Tip 68:** It takes two to get in trouble and one to get blamed.

- **Tip 69:** Detectives carry their own definition of good. Make sure it aligns with Tip 47.

- **Tip 70:** Look up the meaning of "Femme fatales" and "homme fatales." They are deceptively vulnerable and wickedly deceitful.

- **Tip 71:** Detectives live in the gray area of life. Avoid straying into the dark side.

- **Tip 72:** You are never lost if you know where you're headed.

- **Tip 73:** Dream big. Life might spit a drop of opportunity on you.

- **Tip 74:** Stick your neck out for nobody, but sticking out a hand is okay.

- **Tip 75:** Know when to roll credits and end the case. The next one is waiting for you.

The Attitude

A detective's attitude is a weight to carry. Once it settles on you, your body adapts to it. The following fifteen tips will develop you from your inside to your outside.

- **Tip 76:** Be hard-boiled, not soft-boiled. Tough on the inside. Not gooey.

- **Tip 77:** Control your emotions.

- **Tip 78:** It's okay to be afraid if you don't show it.

- **Tip 79:** Be self-confident, not overconfident.

- **Tip 80:** You are different. That's okay. Being different is how you see the differences in others.

- **Tip 81:** Act like you've got nothing to do and a lot of time to do it.

- **Tip 82:** Detectives can be rude. Mothers approve of this if someone makes you feel uncomfortable.

- **Tip 83:** Be a snake charmer among snakes.

- **Tip 84:** Deadpan cynicism. Look up your new favorite detective word. This is your attitude's waterproof makeup.

- **Tip 85:** Today is your day. If you failed yesterday, remember there is always tomorrow.

The Look

Your look reflects your attitude, and it's my favorite part of being a detective. The other tips are more important, but if you want to be taken seriously, follow the next ten tips.

- **Tip 86:** A good smile is the best kind of weapon. Brush your teeth.

- **Tip 87:** Get a coat. One with deep pockets.

- **Tip 88:** Limit your blinking. It allows you to look intense while not missing anything.

- **Tip 89:** Let your eyes gleam like you are a mouse who knows how to get out of a maze.

- **Tip 90:** See the moon in the shine of your shoes.

- **Tip 91:** Fix your face so your emotions don't bleed through.

- **Tip 92:** Stand tall. The size of the mind is stronger than the size of the body.

- **Tip 93:** Sport a proper cockeyed grimace. Practice so you don't look sick.

- **Tip 94:** Homely untidiness needs your assistance. Share the love if you see a citizen in distress.

- **Tip 95:** Master the detective pose—known as the Sam Spade, my idol above idols. Grimace, slouch, pull your coat back and shove your hands in your pockets.

Closing

I've left the indisputable for last. Each one of these tips is a bumper sticker for detectives in training. If you can't handle these, stop reading.

- **Tip 96:** Motivation. Whatever your purpose, make it a good one.

- **Tip 97:** Training is never over.

- **Tip 98:** Facts are on your side.

- **Tip 99:** Some cases are never solved. It doesn't mean you failed.

- **Tip 100:** A good detective's work never turns off.

There you have it. One hundred ways to ensure you are adequately prepared to protect our citizens and stomp out the criminal underworld. Today is the beginning of the rest of your life. Our town's safety relies on your watchful eye. You may not know it, but I'm right there with you. See you around the shadows, Gum Chew.

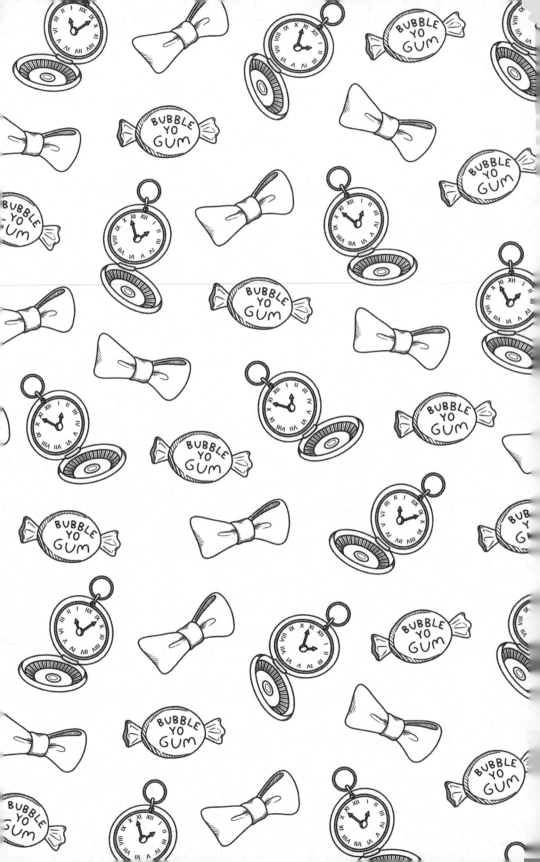